ASHES AND STARS

Also by this author and available
from New English Library:

THE OMEGA POINT

ASHES AND STARS

George Zebrowski

NEW ENGLISH LIBRARY

For Pat LoBrutto, Defender of the faith between Author and Editor

All the characters in this book are fictitious. Any resemblance to actual persons, living or dead, is purely coincidental.

First published in the USA by Ace Books in 1977

First NEL Paperback Edition December 1978

NEL Books are published by
New English Library Limited from
Barnard's Inn, Holborn,
London EC1N 2JR.
Made and printed in Great Britain by
C. Nicholls & Company Ltd.,
The Philips Park Press, Manchester

45004201 4

1. WAR STARS

'But what are kings when regiment is gone,
But perfect shadows in a sunshine day?'
– Marlowe, *Edward the Second*

'The imagination enlarges little objects so as to fill our souls with a fantastic estimate . . .'
– Pascal, *Pensées*

The war stars burned brightly in his memory, each sun a pulsing furnace of hate transforming plasma energies into the frozen grimace of armour, creating the base for war's iron game – machines, weapons, whisper ship hulls – power packaged and stored until the moment of kinetic deployment. There was enough energy here in the Hercules Globular Cluster for a million years of conflict. Some had even dreamed of gathering a hundred stars into a single unit and moving it through space as if it were a ship. No enemy system could have survived a collision with such a configuration.

As he walked down the stony corridor towards the war room located in the centre of the underground base, Gorgias almost smiled at the absurdity of the scheme; but the bitterness set into the muscles of his face resisted even a faint smile. Any culture capable of calling up such a titanic force would have had no need of warfare to gain its ends. Those who had dreamed such dreams had been mad. He imagined the red thread of insanity as a *thing*, a subtle, spidery network of impulses reaching upwards out of some infinitesimal corners of space-time to lace the tender systems of biological structure. Where was the force centre of this willful bestiality, this evil within intelligent beings, so often wished away by well wishers? The radiant energy of the Cluster had poured out with the martial will of its civilization; the suns of home had nurtured an armoury of hate so powerful and tenacious that only the complete destruction of the home worlds had been enough to bring stillness.

Stillness, he thought, but not peace – there was no one to make peace with; New Anatolia and the twenty original worlds of the Empire would be lifeless for tens of thousands of earth years. He felt the flow of hatred in himself, detachment followed by rationality, the silent shock of recognizing one's own workings. He remembered the sense of power that accompanied a noble ancestry, the prideful stance against death; a love of this power struggled to well up inside him and coil around his flesh. But at the same time he felt this strength passing from him, and he was not certain that he would miss it.

Once it might have won against the tall shadows from earth, the pale earthfolk from whose stock the Herculeans had sprung millennia ago, like sparks struck to light new stars. Earthfolk burned more slowly then Herculeans, reasoning, calculating, clinging to their leisure planet in fear of death. Or was this too an illusion?

He thought of his son. What was left for his namesake now? Should he encourage him to settle among the last Herculeans on Myraa's World? Should they continue to go out on nuisance raids against the Earth Federation? Or should they go back into stasis and pass into another time? As if from behind a mask he peered at possibilities beyond the dances of power which had consumed the life of his kind. Together with his son he still lived in the prison of their will; the will which had thrown a net across the stars, pulled together an empire, was ripped open now, lying on cold stones at the bottom of a dark sea.

The lights in the corridor flickered. A returning surge of hatred gripped him as he came to the door of the war room. He stopped and thought of the Whisper Ship lying in its berth in the bowels of the base; he knew what the ship could do, and it was only a matter of time before his son learned also. The base was still an efficient military teaching environment, designed to bring one or a thousand students into full possession of its powers; it was the only school his son had known.

The door opened. Gorgias stepped inside, knowing that he would not try to stop his son; the pressure of the past was too great to permit alternatives, at least any that his son might accept.

In the darkened war room, a haze of projected light stood in a column on the polished surface of the meeting table, casting a three dimensional star map into the space of the large gallery overhead. A long dead, encyclopedic voice was speaking. His son sat on the other side of the large table, a motionless figure staring up at the stars.

Quietly, Gorgias sat down and listened with him.

'Visualize an imaginary translucent tubeway through normal space,' the voice was saying, 'one end attached to Earth's solar system, the other to the Great Globular Cluster in the constellation of Hercules . . .'

Overhead, the image showed the galaxy on edge. A glowing red snake grew out of the solar system, crossing the disc towards the centre in short spirals and arcs until it buried its point in the cluster circling the galactic hub, 34,000 light years from Sol.

'The fastest ships take five earth months to pass through this winding volume of Federation Space, which varies from five to twenty light years in diameter. A hundred thousand worlds circle their suns here, many of them earth-like; others are too young for intelligent life to have developed; some cradle pre-space humanoid cultures; still others have in-system space travel; many are dead worlds. A continuous stream of human life colonizes these worlds, coming out from Earth as well as from other colonial planets. Rejecting engineered environments, this river of life hungers after natural worlds born of suns . . .'

Now it seemed that he was rushing towards the Hercules Cluster at a fantastic speed. The image grew until it took up the whole view, dominating the sky map like a galaxy.

'The greatest object of colonization was the Cluster in Hercules. Its settlement led to a cultural and biological branching of humankind. The biological divergence was accomplished through genetic engineering, specifically through the mixing of human DNA with that of the cluster's original humanoids, whose civilizations contributed much to the style of the emerging Herculean Empire. This hybridization of humankind from Sol led to the greatest recorded conflict in history . . .'

As he looked at the darkened figure of his son, Gorgias thought: brought up in an atmosphere of disintegrating mobilization, pushed along by the pressure of a past he can never rejoin, the young man of two hundred and twenty earth years has grown towards a breaking point; he must recreate the past or die. Inside, his son was a fortress.

Suddenly the lights came on in the gallery, banishing the star maps. The surface of the table below became a lake of light. His son was glaring at him from the far shore.

'I want to hear only one thing from you,' his son said, 'that you will remove Oriona, my mother, your wife, from Myraa's clutches.'

'We can't, you know that – she won't have anything to do with us . . .'

'We will bring her here and she will help us with our plans.'

'Our plans mean nothing to her. How many times do I have to tell you?' *Our plans*, he thought, wondering at how the words now startled him. When had he changed, when had he started thinking differently?

'She'll think differently when she leaves Myraa's influence. Then she'll believe and live as we do . . .'

Once, long ago, Oriona had been his other half in everything. Yes, living on Myraa's World had changed her, probably for the better; she no longer hated the old enemies, she was indifferent to them. Count yourself in, son, Gorgias thought. I'm afraid to say it out loud, but leave me out. What could he say to him that would turn back his natural energy? He looked at his son across the bright table. The black uniform with its orange star of empire was a mirror of his own. There were enough uniforms in the base to clothe a planet.

Characteristically, after a few moments of silence, his son changed the manner of his attack. 'You see, father, we have to be willing to hurt them badly, with small things perhaps, but small things of great cruelty, acts which can never be forgotten, wounds which can never heal. We must hurt them as they hurt us. We can do this.'

'No action we can take against Earth can be decisive, ever.'

'Unless we raise troops and strategic weapons. Meanwhile small sorties will hurt them and preserve our will for a better day.'

'What weapons, what troops? Are you still dreaming of the troop cylinder?'

'There was such a thing towards the end of the war. One day I'll find it.'

'Even a hundred would do no good – at best they stored ten thousand, one division of hastily trained personnel. Even if you found the cylinder, there is no assurance that you could revive those soldiers stored in that way. Actually, I never saw any evidence for the cylinders.'

'But we have the tripod that fits a cylinder here!'

'So maybe there was one – only one.'

'Under good leadership we can grow – the lives in the cylinder are not just for combat.'

'You're talking of committing unborn generations to vengeance. It's over, let it die.' Oriona, you are right, he thought, we must come to the end of our wars; for if we do not, we will not see what lies beyond. What do you see, my love, what is there for you on that green world?

'. . . in your weakness,' his son was saying, 'you fail to see that if we're terrible enough, often enough, we can blackmail a universe.'

Perhaps he was right; what else was there beyond the old war? Inwardly he looked back into the past and saw a black pit far below him . . .

'Only if we remain at large,' he said to his son, 'only if they don't catch us.' The black pit was drawing him down; or was it rushing up to meet him?

'To remain at large is a matter of skill in avoiding a

real test of strength,' his son answered. 'But consider – if we could destroy large populated centres, how long could they deny our demands?'

'You have demands? What in heaven could we ask for that they might not take back later, when we were made harmless?'

'The first demand is recognition of the need to rebuild our home world . . .'

'Sometimes, dear son, I think you're a complete idiot – what can their promises mean after the toll you plan to inflict? Don't you see – any guarantee would be observed by them at their pleasure, not ours.' He looked at his son carefully. Was this the descendant of Gorgias the First, Uniter of Worlds, creator of the Herculean Empire? Perhaps there was more to his son's plan, some shrewdness he had missed.

'We would keep a hidden strike force. At the first violation we make them pay! If we can remain at large, you and I, then so could such a force.'

Gorgias felt his head shake in denial, as if it had become independent of his body; his right hand trembled and for a moment he was unable to speak. His son's will had entered him and taken possession, half convincing him, remdinding him of his own earlier self, with its resolve and hatred. All that would be required to make his son's terrible vision work was an iron terror, a will that would be ready to do anything against the enemy, a resolve that would not crumble when confronted by pity. This would be the game Oriona feared, the iron game that would set father and son in the service of an old hatred, turning them into devices to serve the dead. Father and son had skirted the edge of this game; now, finally, they would be drawn into its merciless logic and cruel satisfactions . . .

'One day,' his son continued, 'our worlds will be

repopulated, our power rebuilt. We will have little need of threats then. But until then, you and I must be guardians of that future. Have you forgotten? Have you become a coward? Won't you even try – or will you abandon me as you abandoned Oriona?'

Gorgias looked into his son's eyes. *I won't need you*, they seemed to say, *I'll become my own father, I'll deny you if you refuse me and you'll be left alone. Without Oriona and me you are nothing.* A shuddering fear, like breaking metal, passed through him. He tasted its cold in his mouth. His stomach knotted in rage, and he knew for the first time that he would be able to kill his own son – if for no other reason than to abolish this monstrous resurgence of his own youth, this fortress self which had come out of him, out of the past, to stand alone in this way.

Oriona's eyes looked at him from beneath black eyebrows and black hair. 'Well?' his son asked. 'Will you plan with me?' The questions were now shouts, strong and insistent and convinced, assuming agreement. For a moment his son's shouting shape seemed to become a torso rising from the frozen lake of the polished surface, an awesome creature imprisoned here by the sheer weight of its own hatred, its own strength turned against itself until time faded its vitality. His son was a creature of loveless power, making him doubt again, forcing him to feel once more the uncoiling insanity of the failed past.

'All right,' Gorgias said softly, 'but first –'

'Good!'

'– but first we'll visit Oriona.' Perhaps she may be able to quiet her son, he thought, even though the life she lives is a delusion.

'We'll take her away,' his son said.

'Let's see how she feels.' A lie might save his son's

life. Any delay might change the future; for once his son started on this new course, there would be no turning back; his life would become a hunted thing, and one day his son would die. Any delay might save him. There were worlds aplenty outside the Federation, where a life might be started anew; a small community . . . simply existing . . . perhaps Oriona was living that life right now.

'I'll prepare the ship,' his son said.

Gorgias nodded and tried to quiet himself, turning inwards as one who seeks refuge from a coming storm.

2. JUMPSPACE

'It is natural for the mind to believe, and for the will to love; so that, for want of true objects, they must attach themselves to false.'

– Pascal, *Pensées*

'A man knew himself as the product of this world. He sought to become its consciousness: a way of dreaming that would embody its salvation.'

– Bousquet

A shadowed face floated in the stone ceiling, and faded; in another moment it would have spoken to him.

Cave eyes stared at a barrier of ice in a timeless place.

Outside the black walls, floor and ceiling of the doorless room lay an infinite solidity; the cell was the only open space, cut miraculously out of a universe of rigid substance. The lonely lamp in the corner at his right would go out if he looked away; the darkness would flow in around him and solidify, freezing his movement until his flesh also turned stony . . .

The home world lay before him. He had never seen it after the holocaust, yet suddenly he was there. The land was an endless plain of ashes, the remains of cities and towns, the very mountains. The planet was a heated dust bowl, wind whipped and sterile. Grief held back all his tender reactions, all regret and tears. He felt the hell wind on his face, tasted the baked ash in his mouth as the grey sea drifted around his feet.

He walked forward across the meadow of ashes. The horizon was a wavy line of heat distortions. He came abruptly to a large circular pit in the waste; stars burned below the world, glowing gravel floating in a subterranean universe . . .

The dream was always the same.

A titanic fist pounded on the wall behind his bed, making the stone echo like metal; the black surfaces of the room became glassy and shattered, flowing away like water . . .

He sat up suddenly and saw his father standing in the open doorway.

'Are you awake?'

'I'm ready,' he said, feeling distrustful of the silhouette blocking the flow of light into his quarters. His father's dark shape turned and went out into the corridor.

He looked at the dark lamp in the corner, remembering that in the dream he had believed that his life was somehow dependent on its continued shining; a curious absurdity.

He got up and prepared to follow his father to the ship.

The ramp tunnel exit loomed ahead suddenly and the whisper ship shot out over the barren surface of the planet. A glowing cloud of interstellar gas blazed from horizon to horizon as the vessel raced over jagged mountains, stone filled valleys and dusty plains; airless, beaten by solar wind and heat, the lifeless world orbited faithfully, forever dead in the angry glare of its small, white hot primary. Located near the centre of the cluster, the entire system was wrapped in a cloud of gas and dust one-half light year across.

The ship lifted into the shining sky. Variations in

cloud density let in the light of cluster stars, the glow fading as the ship shifted position.

With his father now asleep in the aft quarters, the younger Gorgian began his first watch. Without warning the ship slipped into otherspace, revealing the stars of the cluster as perfectly round black coals set at an indefinite distance. For the next one hundred and fifty hours the ship would push through this ashen sea, 50,000 light years across the top of the galaxy, halfway across the spiral, past where the earth swam deep in the spiral disc's outer arms, upwards to the sparsely starred region where Myraa's World looked out on the dark between the galaxies.

All through his first watch, the younger Gorgias was irritated by the shroud of hyperspace covering the known universe, hiding the diamond hard stars, abolishing the black void's comfort, leaving only the ash-white continuum dotted with the obsidian analogs of objects in normal space-time. The bones of reality, he thought, dry and lifeless; passing through this region was always a slow dying.

Did he really care about the Herculean dead? He searched himself, trying to feel the death of millions. The killing of ten would have been intolerable. Each of those hundreds of millions would have lived a thousand earth years or more, each life an entire world of experience, now cut off. To remember their passing was to deny oneself all normal day to day living, all simplicity, all love; to remember their passing was to act in ways that would change him irrevocably, making him an instrument, a sacrifice to the fires of outrage. He did not, and never would, belong to himself, or to anyone else.

If he could hurt even ten earthborn, the news would

humiliate millions; the dead deserved that much. Each blow, however small, would be a reminder that the Federation's victory had not been complete. The dead were alive within him, sparks ready to flare up into an inner fire; his strength was the needed fuel; his strength was their will preparing to live again. Rest would come for him only when all the hatred he bore was spent.

The thought of his father's growing weakness made him angry again. He felt it as a coldness camped at his centre, a promise of failure. He would have wanted to have left the older man in stasis at their last waking and gone out by himself, but the ship was still tuned to the other's personality and would obey no one else. The ship could only be his by deliberate transfer of command by the owner; his father's death would not give him the ship. He needed his father's good will.

If only a second Whisper Ship could be found. Perhaps there was one somewhere on Myraa's World. He had always suspected that Myraa knew more than she was willing to tell. Maybe he could learn something from Oriona. Myraa or one of the other survivors might have revealed something to her, a piece of information that would not appear to be useful, but which might be crucial to one who could fit it into a larger context. The visit might turn out to be useful after all.

He found himself thinking about Myraa – her nakedness, her long hair, her smile, the freshness of her skin. Thoughts of her always brought out his weakest feelings. The universe of time and space had cheated him (what was this *effort* of time passing?) of the simplest pleasures enjoyed by the humblest creatures on a million worlds. He was a thinking, self-conscious *object* living in a plenum where *distance* lay between objects that were made up of infinitesimally spaced small objects lying below gross perception. What was justice, or vengeance, in such a universe? Why did he crave closeness with Myraa, and why was he compelled to believe that distance from her way of life was necessary for him? In his way he loved her, but he would not give himself up to her; the cry of the past was stronger than her love; for him to ignore the past would be to die.

He would have to recreate the history from which he sprang; it would have to be a certain kind of living object, a network of conscious beings again holding the Hercules Cluster together. To this community he would give himself; there love might not be a fault; there he would shine as he had been meant to shine, a king from a line of kings; there he would know the past and future as they should be, unshattered and filled with the meaning of time; there the past would be pride, the future a distant glowing goal that would consume all things in its crucible of satisfaction and joy.

On the screen, the desolation of otherspace promised nothing as the ship rushed through its oblivion.

When his father came in to take his first watch period, Gorgias stood up and let the older man take the station chair.

'I've found a likely target for us,' Gorgias said.

His father swung the seat around and glared at him. The face was pale, the blue eyes sunken from worry and doubt; the hands sought each other from fear, then pushed apart to hide the fact. 'What are you talking about? We were not to plan anything until after the visit.'

'Thirty light years south of Myraa there is a frontier world, mostly small towns, not more than half a million people, an easy target.'

His father gripped the armrests. 'Later, we don't have time to discuss it now, get some rest.'

'You said you would fight –'

'A world that size is unimportant, settled by rejects. Federation won't be impressed.'

'We could destroy a town in a single run.'

'They'd look for us on Myraa's World immediately. They could hold Oriona and others hostage . . .'

'We could do it after we take Oriona with us. Besides, what makes you so sure they are capable of holding hostages? My studies show that they are too cowardly to try such a tactic.'

His father was shaking his head. 'There's too little thought and preparation. Don't be so impatient. Do you think that Federation military operatives are stupid? They'll pick up on every mistake. They won the war that way.'

'But they never came up against a Whisper Ship.'

'True, the ship is unassailable, but you might imprison yourself forever inside. Even the life support systems require mass to synthesize food . . .'

'I could recycle indefinitely.'

'But you would starve if something went wrong. Son, there are ways to trap or disrupt the ship. In time it would be possible to bring enough power to bear on it to tear it open.'

'Things would never get that far,' Gorgias said. He turned and started aft, determined not to continue the discussion.

'Rest well,' his father called after him just as the bulkhead door slid shut. There was no point in angering the old man now. Later, he thought, when the ship is mine, I can do as I wish, but I need him now to control the ship's programmes. Suddenly he feared that his father would never relinquish control of the ship. He searched for a hypothetical solution to that problem, returning quickly to the original belief that the vessel would be his in time; whatever his father's short term doubts, the old man would not betray his own son.

At the end of the short corridor, another door slid open to let him into the aft quarters, containing a large bunk with gravity controls, bath cubicle and a small kitchen dispenser.

Gorgias lay down on the bunk and tried to sleep, struggling to reach a deep calm, but rest charged a toll of memory before releasing him into its quietest realm. He was on Myraa's World for the first time. 'Is this home?' he asked his father. No, it was another place, far from their enemies. Here the surviving Herculeans might live in peace. A green field showed a pit, a wound cut in the grass. Bodies lay in the pit, the corpses of Herculean animals, those that had been unable to adjust to the new planet. Later fleeing warships had arrived, burning the grass into desert with their makeshift jets; only the crudest planetfall was left to them after their strained gravitics had failed.

Spring light was streaming through Myraa's window, beams walking ghostly on the floor. Whole ships had been gutted to build the house on the hill. Sickness, suicide and lack of provisions had decimated the survivors, soldier and specialist alike; no hand or brain remained now that could repair, operate, or even understand the dead fleet. Only the Whisper Ship ran itself, demanding little direct understanding of its systems for effective operation.

Beams of steel passed through his body, pinning him in a place beyond sleep. There was no pain and no possibility of movement; in a few moments there would be . . . nothing.

He woke up and listened to the perfect silence of the cabin, imagining that the cold wintriness of hyperspace was increasing, pressing in on the ship, and would soon lock it into immobility within the grey continuum. The cabin smelled of cold metal. He closed his eyes again and thought of entering stasis for . . . a thousand . . . two thousand years. Would the Federation still exist after ten thousand years? Would the machines maintain the stasis field for that long? What kind of universe would he come out into after a million years? No revenge would be possible for him in that universe. To step into it would require no more than a subjective moment of sleep, and all his purpose would be left behind. The idea filled him with a sense of loss. He saw himself going alone across time, the past a black pit behind him; but there was a pull in that abyss, and it drew him backwards, pulling him closer each time he fell asleep; one day he would not wake in time to save himself.

Then all thoughts and dreams left him, as he knew they would, as they always had; but again he wondered if he had won, or if a tide had simply gone out.

During his second watch he saw the ship's ghost on the screen, running ahead at a fixed distance. He wondered if an insubstantial copy of himself was sitting before the screen in the phantom vessel, watching a still more distant illusion, and if his father was resting in the after quarters there also.

When he slept again after his watch, the ship turned to glass, letting in the ghastly grey-white light from beyond, the glow of an overcast creation, or the underside of a universe forever turned away from the living.

Eyes closed, he stared into the distance, believing that he was on an ocean in fog, with a city's lights showing on the far horizon. Around him the sea swam with leviathans and fire-fly fish.

Opening his eyes, he longed for starlight, for sight of worlds, for living things. He looked at his hands. His skin was growing pale here, as if the few days had really been years. What was time in jumpspace? Perhaps a long time was lost in transit, then regained at the moment of exit, leaving in the traveller only the memory of long imprisonment.

He closed his eyes again. Memory was bare and clean, as stony as the halls and chambers of the base. He felt pity for himself, for his father, for Oriona imprisoned on Myraa's World, for his brother who had died there. Only revenge was left; nothing else would fill him up completely and quiet his hunger; nothing else would lead to the constructive plan of renewal for his people. The only way to redeem the past was to bring it into the present and use it to control the future; he had to make memory a material thing, a force that would lash out at the earthborn, making it impossible for them to ignore his demands. Revenge was the only way to kindle recognition in those who had taken everything from him, leaving this grey present, an old man and a black future.

If I do not reach out to hurt, he thought, I will not want to live.

A shadowed face looked down at him, and he knew that he would cease to be if it turned its gaze away. Again the pit of things past pulled him in, closer this time; he reached for a handhold to keep himself from falling in, but he woke up before he could grasp it.

3. EXILES

'The liberty of the individual is no gift of civilization.'

– Freud

'There is nothing worse for mortal men than wandering.'

– Homer, *The Odyssey*

The ashes of jumpspace faded; the black coals caught fire and became bright stars again. Nearby, the sun of Myraa's World burned with a yellow-orange life, its shouting light filling the screen, humbling the observer who had just emerged from limbo.

I have reached the complexity of hating myself, the older Gorgias thought. My son will begin to hate me and I will not want to live. I am not sure that his plans will be ineffective, I have simply lost . . . my taste for war. Reproaches rose in his brain, the dark shapes of Herculean soldiers going into battle, each one crying out for him to remember his training, his loyalty, the meaning of cowardice and treason. I am not guilty, he said to the shapes, everything has changed.

Myraa's World grew large on the screen until it took up the whole view. The ship cut into the atmosphere and circled halfway around the planet before dropping to a few kilometres above the ocean.

His son came in and stood behind him as the screen showed sight of land ahead. The water below grew shallow, revealing sunlit bottom. In a few moments the ship was past the rocky beach and rushing low over the land.

Oriona. He wondered how she would greet him this time. How would she greet her son? Would she continue to judge in her silent way? If she spoke to him, what would he say to her, what could he say to her after thirty years? She had lived those years while he had stolen them – stolen them from her and from himself. He would not see those years in her face; few Herculeans below the age of five hundred showed signs of age.

The ship turned north, running over worn mountains and grassy valleys. The yellow afternoon sunlight stained the greenery, making it look blue in patches.

'We're almost there,' his son said quietly, almost as if he were afraid.

We're almost home, the older man thought. It always surprised him to think of Myraa's World as home; in a way it was home, the gathering place of almost all remaining Herculeans; it was home because Oriona was here, and because he was here with his son, however brief the visit; it was home because his son had once asked him if it was home, and he had lied.

The hill and house came into view. A circular design of panoramic windows drank in the western sunlight, though some shade was provided by six elegant trees standing in a carpet of tall grass. He saw that the trees were taller, their trunks larger. The branches were thicker with the curving needles, and the red cones were as bright as the gem sands of New Anatolia's beaches.

The ship circled once and landed in a hover at the bottom of the hill in back of the house, where the evening shadow would cloak it.

He turned and looked at his son, but there was no sign of shared feelings in the younger man's face. For a moment Gorgias was afraid that his son would guess his state of mind and see it as yet another sign of weakness, but the other was already turning away to leave the ship.

He got up and followed his son out of the control room to the side lock. The mechanism had already cycled and they stepped out into a warm south wind which greeted them with the scent of living things. The effect was almost a shock after the sterility of the base and jumpspace.

The hill was a thirty degree climb on a dirt footpath. His son reached the door first and waited. They stood together for a minute until the door opened. Inside, they walked to the front room through a narrow corridor.

'There's no one here,' his son said as they passed by the open bedroom door.

The black floor was dustless, as if someone had just cleaned it. The chairs sat alone facing the massive bowed windows, waiting for those who would come out of time to seat themselves; the silence seemed eternal.

'Welcome.'

They both turned and saw Myraa standing in front of the entrance to the corridor. She wore a simple blue robe which matched her eyes. A hood hid her long brown hair.

'Welcome,' she repeated, 'I knew you were coming.'

She could not have known, he thought, but it gives her a sense of power to say that she did.

'Where's Oriona?' his son asked.

Myraa took a few steps into the room and said, 'Oriona is no longer living –'

The sentence stopped for an eternity, preventing him from hearing the rest.

'– as you know it. It was her wish.'

His son went up to her. 'Wish? What are you talking about? How did it happen – an accident? Was she murdered?'

'It was her wish,' Myraa said. 'She left nothing for you, and she does not want to speak with you now.'

'What are you saying?' his son asked. 'Tell me where she is – is she dead or not?'

'She exists elsewhere, whether you accept it or not. I am telling you this so that you will calm yourself.'

His son turned to him. 'What is she saying?'

'Their belief is that, well – people are absorbed into others, like herself, becoming multiple personalities. I've never paid the idea much attention. Oriona is dead – Myraa is trying to . . . excuse me.' He closed his eyes and felt a warmth spread through his body. He felt his head bow and a freezing weakness entered his muscles. He recovered and opened his eyes. 'Myraa is trying to sugar coat the fact,' he finished. Turning, he sat down in the nearest chair and looked out the window.

Behind him, he heard his son strike Myraa across the face.

'Liar! What has happened?'

'I've told you,' Myraa said, and there was no anger in her voice.

'Suicide?'

'No, but it was her wish.'

'Do you hear yourself – which was it?'

'You've heard the truth.'

'Explain it to me.'

'She who was your mother lives . . . in a different way.'

Oriona, the older Gorgias said to himself as he looked

out the curving window, *now only your name is left to me*. A gust of wind shook the tree near the house, hurling a few red cones against the window in front of him.

'You'll tell me,' his son was saying, 'you'll tell me what you mean.'

Stillness returned to the room, as if time had run backwards to the moment when they had come in.

Then he heard a rush of air and a thud. He turned and saw that his son had kicked Myraa in the stomach. She lay on the floor, clutching her belly without a sound. He gave her a disgusted nudge with his boot, turned and sat down in the other chair facing the window.

'Where are the others, I wonder,' his son said loudly, 'maybe they'll know more.' Turning to look at him, his son asked, 'Is she raving?'

'Maybe Oriona's death has affected her. Did you think before you hit her?'

'You didn't try to stop me.'

I can't stop you from doing anything, he thought. He closed his eyes and turned his head away to keep his son from seeing the tears threatening to well out of his eyes. *Oriona*, he said to himself, almost singing the name. *So few, so few Herculeans left.*

'What is it?' his son asked.

'Just tired.' *Oriona, Oriona, I'll never see you again. All that might have changed between us is now impossible. How could that have been taken from us?*

He opened his eyes and turned to his son. 'Go pick her up – apologize.'

Suddenly the younger man laughed, and a look of contempt came into his eyes. 'Apologize? For what? You've lost your mind. She lives here and does nothing but invent lies! We have only her word that Oriona is dead.'

Alive – maybe she was somewhere outside walking, nothing more. In a moment he would get up and go find her. Then he realized how long it would be before he accepted her death; the slightest hope was a shock, pushing him into wish-fulfillment.

'I pity you both,' Myraa said from the floor.

She sounds like Oriona.

'Dear father, we should be preparing for war!'

'At least her lies keep alive the few of us who are left.'

'You and I live without her.'

'She keeps the Federation from killing those who stay with her.'

'How – by being meek and cowardly? They could all be killed in a few minutes.'

'Then why haven't they done it?'

'The earthborn are fools,' his son said, 'nothing more.'

'Then being humble is a way to survive, is it not?'

His son did not reply further. Myraa got up and came to stand between them. 'Look,' she said as she gazed out the window.

Wearily, the older man got up and stepped to the window; his son joined him.

At the bottom of the hill, a procession was starting to make its way up to the house, thirty people marching single file with hands linked. Each wore the black body garment of the Herculean military, but with no insignia. A body without a head, the older Gorgias thought, but they live while their leaders rot.

'What are they doing?' his son asked.

As he watched the human chain coming up the hill, the older Herculean thought of escape.

'They are your brothers and sisters,' Myraa said. 'All that your mother was is mirrored within them. She is more alive than ever.'

'Idiotic nonsense,' his son said.

Escape, the old Herculean thought. To leave all known worlds behind, to go outside the narrow corridor of worlds strung between earth and the cluster . . .

'It's true,' Myraa said.

He thought of the worlds nearest earth, where power for work was plentiful, where the only problem of life was in what to do with one's time. There the problems of longevity were directing a different form of natural selection, one in which only the most ingenious and creative individuals would survive into advanced ages, beyond the one thousand year mark, while the rest died of accident and ennui. He remembered his raids against a number of those worlds just after the war's end, when his infant son and Oriona were hiding on the planet which later came to be called Myraa's World. He remembered the contempt he had felt for the long lived, useless earthpeople he had seen. He had disliked killing these temporal drifters. A pair of eyes, a face, an expression of vacant worry – images of various individuals still lived inside him. Too many had seemed content to die. He wondered if long life gave powerful individuals a proprietary view of reality; maybe it had something to do with the war and with military ambitions on both sides . . .

Vaguely he noticed that his son was about to strike Myraa again. She retreated from him and his son followed until they were behind him. He heard the blow, followed by two dull sounds. Myraa and his son were struggling on the floor. Children, he thought. Myraa would show her strength now, as she had done when they had both been children long ago . . .

He thought of worlds further out in the Federation corridor, worlds teeming with colonists who had burned and reseeded whole planets. There life was more dangerous, yet death was not as feared as among the long lived; but still the ties with the interior worlds were strong, since so many skills and services emanated from earth . . .

Behind him Gorgias and Myraa were quiet at last, but he did not turn his chair to look at them.

He thought of the fringe worlds of the corridor, scarcity ridden places where earth was almost unknown. Into this far end had come the ships of the Cluster, building, consolidating, gathering loyalty at the most distant nerve ends of earth's influence; for in fact it was from these most distant worlds that his people were descended, having grown powerful within the rich environment of closely spaced suns inside Hercules.

Later had come the ambition of pushing through to earth itself, of taking the entire corridor, 50,000 light years of space and worlds, for the Cluster. The introversion of earth's stratified immortalist society was supposed to have guaranteed victory. Herculean immortals had needed something grand to do with their existence, he thought.

But earth had come to care. The takeover of the outer words had taken too long; one by one the outer worlds began to fight back furiously, and this led to the waking of the earthgiant. His waking response brought back all that was strong and alert and clever in his nature, the same qualities that had built the largest human civilization in history, including Hercules. He had come breathing fire against Cluster worlds, until New Anatolia was burned into a cinder and all hope of winning against him became a sad joke.

Slowly he turned and saw that Myraa and his son were no longer in the room with him. Later, he knew, his son's rage would return, regardless of Myraa's efforts to quiet him; with Oriona gone, he saw no hope for his son.

He got up and wandered the large room, thinking about the possibility of life beyond the Earth-Hercules corridor; the corridor was only a thin thread of intelligence lacing the galaxy. Maybe there were other cultures in the central regions of the disc. Was there enough lure in the idea to interest his son? There had to be a way to change his plans, even if it was with the false hope of making his son think those same plans possible.

'How nice, father,' he imagined his son saying, '– you want me to become an explorer. For whom shall we explore, to what end shall we contact other civilizations? Behind me stands the ghost of a dead civilization. Shall we do it for them?'

Then, after a long silence, his son would continue, half believing. 'Will they give us the power to revive our civilization, father?'

'Perhaps,' he would answer.

'Why should they, whoever they are? And did you consider that we may be alone, that there are no greater civilizations in the galaxy? Even if they exist, they might not wish to be found . . .'

The oldest living Herculean sat down in the chair again. Outside, the procession had reached the house and was now standing in front of the windows, peaceful faces looking in. He did not know any of them, and they gave no sign of knowing him.

There was dirt on their hands. He wondered if they had come from burying Oriona somewhere out there in the tall grass of the hilly countryside. They were too polite to come into the house, knowing that he was here with his son. He thought of them living in their monastic cells inside the hill beneath the house; there each occupant turned away from the universe of light and colour and substance, in the name of seeing past life and death to some fabulous yonder. They might just as easily see through their cell walls, he thought bitterly. Reality lay not in their self-generated ecstasies, but in the cold ground of worms and decomposition outside their cells; in the life giving ruin of nature which never gave the same thing twice, settling instead for a repetition of types and approximations, none exactly like the other; in the endless processes of star formation and universe construction, not in the wishes of creatures caught between the infinitesimally small and the infinitely large . . .

Oriona. The thought of her pulsed inside him like a beating heart. His returning grief threatened to swell up inside him and tear his body apart. Ignoring the faces outside, he leaned forward in the chair and put his face in his hands, rubbing his eyes until they exploded into a storm of colours. At any moment he would fall back into the past; his eyes would fail to open when he took his hands away and he would be a stranger to his body while his mind drifted amongst the bloody images of war, in a limbo of sharp pains and shabby sights . . .

Suddenly Oriona stood in his blind sight, as if thrown up to him by a merciful field of creation. Naked and beautiful, she stood with her legs together, hands folded across her breasts, eyes looking directly at him, long black hair flowing in a mysterious wind . . .

He cried out and opened his eyes; the afterimage faded on the window before him and he was looking again at the mourners outside.

Oriona, he said to her memory, *your son will go out to kill now, and I am powerless to stop him; he is as I was, and will be again to help him.* Then a distant thought whispered itself to him: *if you died he would change*. And an even closer whisper hissed inside him: *you could kill him.*

As if something had spoken to them, the mourners outside turned and made their way down the hill, again holding hands in a chain of black figures.

4. SORTIE

'The passion for destruction is also a creative passion.'

– Bakunin

'Life is impoverished, it loses in interest, when the highest stake in the game of living, life itself, may not be risked . . . [in war] Death will no longer be denied; we are forced to believe in it. People really die; and no longer one by one . . . thousands in a single day. Life . . . has recovered its full content.'

– Freud

After their bodies were quiet, Gorgias opened his eyes and watched Myraa as she slept next to him. There was no other woman for him among the survivors; she would know him as the son of leaders, to whom the future belonged even if that future were lost.

Lost. For a moment he considered what it would be like to come and live here with Myraa, but the thought shamed him; he felt weak before it. He must never forget that something greater had been taken from him.

Myraa opened her eyes and he smiled at her.

'Do you understand now,' she started to ask, 'that your mother –'

He turned away from her. 'Stop telling me crazy stories – they may help you but they do not calm me. Why don't you just tell me what happened?'

'When she was ready for passage, she did it herself.'

'What?' He turned to face her, angry again. He had been getting ready to apologize for striking her, but that was again impossible for him. 'What did it take to convince a mature woman to take her own life?'

'But she's not dead –'

'Then where is she?'

'Right here – looking at you through my eyes. One day, when you come to understand, she will speak. The passage she has taken –'

He hit her across the face with the back of his hand. She rolled away from him and lay on her back, saying nothing. He got up, put on his black uniform and boots, and went out into the main room where his father still sat looking out the windows. Gorgias went to the window and looked out into the start of twilight. He saw the group waiting at the bottom of the hill.

'What do the fools want?'

'They've come from burying Oriona, I think.'

'Where?'

'Somewhere out there in the tall grass.'

'Then she is dead, no matter what Myraa says.'

His father looked up at him suddenly. 'What did she tell you?'

'That Oriona is alive inside her and will speak to us one day.'

A look of naive hope entered his father's pale face.

'Don't be stupid,' Gorgias said, 'you're a fool and not my father if you believe any of it. They're mad here, comforting themselves with lies and stories – anything to forget.'

'I agree, don't think I take it seriously.'

'They talked Oriona into believing it also. Oriona killed herself!'

The older Herculean stood up. 'Myraa said this?'

'Just a few minutes ago she tried to talk me into their madness. We've got to go. My way is the only way.'

His father was silent.

Gorgias looked outside and saw that the mourners had disappeared. He turned again to his father and said, 'Don't you see – our defeat in the war created all this. Myraa and all the others are this way because of the war. Oriona's death is the fault of the earthborn. We must strike back, we must make them feel our punishment in any way open to us. When will you share the ship with me?'

His father looked directly at him but did not answer. The knitted brows seemed to be crushing the blue eyes peering out of the haggard face; his arms were pressed against the stocky body, hands closed into fists. Then the wrinkles on the forehead relaxed, leaving a smooth surface.

Gorgias turned in triumph and started for the back door, knowing that the weakness he had just seen in his father's face was a guarantee that he would soon surrender the ship to his son. The vessel was for those who had the courage to use it as its great designers had intended – for war.

When his son came out from Myraa's sleeping room, a wave of pity and fear passed through the older Herculean. He watched his son come to the window and look down at the burial party still gathered at the bottom of the hill.

'What do the fools want?'

'They've come from burying Oriona.'

'Where?' his son asked.

'Somewhere out there in the grass.'

'Then she is dead, no matter what Myraa says.'

He looked up at his son and asked, 'What did she tell you?'

'That Oriona is inside her and will speak to us one day.'

Could it be true, he wondered, was such a gathering of life after this life possible? If so, then immortality was a foolish thing. He thought of his vision of Oriona. Was she trying to reach him? Herculean women had been known for psionic abilities. Fool, he told himself suddenly, there is no evidence for anything like this; the universe had always been unfair and uncaring of wishes. Hope could not create life, or extend it into the void . . .

'Don't be stupid,' his son said, 'you're a fool if you believe any of it. They're mad . . . comforting themselves with lies and stories . . .'

'I agree,' he said mechanically, 'don't think I take it seriously.' *And what lies do you live by, my son*, he said to himself, knowing that they were the ones he had once believed himself.

'They talked Oriona into believing it also. Oriona killed herself!'

He stood up. 'Myraa said this?' Then he remembered that she had said it before, but neither of them had taken it literally.

'. . . Oriona's death is the fault of the earthborn,' his son was saying . . . 'when will you share the ship with me?'

He felt a sudden anger in himself, triggered by his son's demand for the ship; anger at Myraa and Oriona; anger at himself for not being able to regain his old strength; anger at the pitiless tide that washed from past to future and had left him here on this despairing shore.

His son turned and left the room. The back door opened and closed with a terrible finality; such a small thing to mark the moment of his surrender to his son's will.

Surrender? They would lash out together, bringing a piece of the cruel past into the life of the Federation. There would be a public recognition of the past, however small; there was satisfaction in the thought, and he realized that this was how his son felt all the time. He would transfer control of the ship to his son as soon as possible.

He started across the room towards the hall leading to the back exit, but stopped when something reached into him, filling him with sudden doubt and panic. *Oriona, forgive me*, he thought, *but there is nothing left for me. I cannot live without my son's approval. I have no one else now.*

He went through the hall. Myraa's naked shape lay on the bed, her body a deep blue from the twilight streaming in the east window. He stopped as she sat up and looked at him, then he hurried to the back door.

It opened and he stepped outside and went down the hill to where the Whisper Ship waited in a warm evening.

His father stood by his side, his face a mask as they watched grey jumpspace swallow Myraa's World. A reflection of them appeared on the screen for a moment, the ghostly images of two mournful men standing in an infinite sepulchre, faces in shadow. Then the black ghosts that marked star positions appeared, and Gorgias felt again as if he were returning to a vast universe of the dead lying beneath or alongside a continuum of colour and life. Here death might dance with his will, fear make love to his courage and dream assassins slaughter his capacity for hope, if he stayed too long . . .

'I'll match the ship to you,' his father said.

The older Herculean had come to his senses at last, Gorgias thought as he sat down in the station.

His father reached past him and touched the pressure panel. A sequence of numbers appeared on the screen, overlaying the view of subspace.

'The ship will know you by this number. If you ever have to assign the ship to another, you must cancel this number and invent a new one, as I have just done. The ship's internal fields will adjust to your body and brain wave signatures within a day. If these are absent from the ship's interior for any great length of time, and you have left no instructions, the ship will destruct. Remember this.'

'I will, father, I will . . .'

The board went dark and the numbers faded from the screen as the older man withdrew his hand.

It's mine, Gorgias thought.

'When we come out of hyperspace, you will be in command. Congratulations, Captain.'

'Thank you, Sir.'

The older man turned and went aft, leaving him alone.

The oldest Herculean dreamed the past. It drew him into itself, to feel and live again. He was running down a long corridor with Oriona. The passage was filled with water to their ankles; the damp smell of sewage almost made them gag. The air was growing hotter as the city above them went through the stages of disintegration from massive laser fire.

High above the planet, mobile fortresses the size of planetoids lanced energy into New Anatolia, incinerating whole cities, precipitating whirlwinds and earthquakes; floodwaters were crossing continents as the polar caps melted.

'Just ahead,' he said, pushing his wife ahead. 'There, it's there – where the General said he'd left it.'

They came to the hidden Whisper Ship, the last possibility of retreat for a group of officers now dead, a gift of mercy for himself and Oriona.

'Our child will live,' Oriona shouted as they scrambled into the side lock. It cycled behind them as they went forwards into the control area.

'It's preset for its base,' he said as he took the station chair.

'Is that safe?' she asked.

'It'll switch to jumpspace in the atmosphere, and it's faster than Federation craft.' He touched the plate and fed in the numbers given to him by the General. Images of the streets above them persisted in his mind – metal flowing down from the melting upper levels; people dying from the sudden heat, exploding as steam formed from the water of their bodies; level after level collapsing as crowds fled downwards. In less than a day the heat would sink the city, and dozens of others, into the planet.

The earthgiant had come well prepared, with a large fleet escorting hundreds of brute power units. The approach of this armada had drawn all Herculean forces back to defend the Cluster. It was clear now that those forces would not be enough to save New Anatolia or any of the Cluster worlds.

The Whisper Ship rushed out of the drain tunnel – into a sky of red dust. Columns of energy pushed down from the sky, one for each city and town of the hemisphere. The atmosphere was blue around the frozen bolts as they pumped power into the screaming planet . . .

'Stop it!'

A hand struck him across the face. He opened

his eyes to see his ten-year-old son bending over him.

'Stop it!'

'The dream?'

'It hurts – it's so terrible.'

His son was receiving his nightmares. The effect was not as violent as it was for Oriona, but it was bad enough.

'I'll wake up and it will be better,' he said, 'we'll take a walk down the hill . . .'

Then he opened his eyes again and found himself floating in the aft quarters of the ship. Time had rushed by; the boy of ten was a man; Oriona was dead; and when the ship came out of jumpspace, his son would be in command.

Thirty light years south of Myraa's World, the Whisper Ship stabbed into the atmosphere of Precept, a frontier world near the end of the Federation's other corridor, a volume of space that was slowly being settled in the direction of the galactic rim.

The younger Gorgias knew that the thickening atmosphere outside the hull was beginning to howl from the vessel's intrusion, and there would be thunderclaps and vortices when the ship levelled off near the surface.

The screen showed swirling clouds and fleeting glimpses of brown and green surface. His father came into the cabin and stood silently behind him. Abruptly the clouds cleared and the ship was running level with the country below.

'How is it going?' his father asked. 'Do you have to talk to the ship much?'

'Very well – no, it pretty much guesses what I want it to do. The programme plate is enough.'

'You can override it with your voice, or add instructions.'

'I'm well aware of that.'

The first settlement became visible far ahead, a scattering of domes and primitive wooden dwellings on an open plain. There were few signs of vegetation inside the town. As the ship approached, groups of people looked up, toy figures on a dirt tabletop. A few were waving.

Automatically, the forward laser cannon lashed out with its tongue, flitting from one structure to the next; one by one, buildings began to blaze. In a few moments the ship was past and circling for a repeat run.

The cannon widened its beam and caught all remaining structures. The tabletop town was slowly being cloaked in black smoke. The ship shot past and circled again.

'What do you think?' Gorgias asked his father without turning around.

His father did not reply.

'You think this is too easy, and you're right. But the object is to hurt them, give them something to talk about, not fight a textbook battle.'

As the ship continued to circle, Gorgias turned around in his station and glared at his father. 'How many dead do you think?'

'This is not warfare.'

'So – it comes out again! You wouldn't have said that once. Why do you care so much about being fair now? My point is not so obscure – there is no defence against the unthinkable.'

'But you can't win unless you can escalate terrorism into conventional conflict – destruction of Federation industry, and then invasion. You can't win . . .'

'I'm not planning to win. How many times do I have

to say it? I want to hurt them, make them know that we live and remember.'

'And you want to continue with that indefinitely?'

'Who's to say that we won't find wider support later,' Gorgias said as an afterthought.

'I don't want to argue – I'm here, that should be enough for you.'

The older man turned and left the cabin.

Gorgias shrugged and turned back to the screen. On the plain below, the smoke was a billowing, churning darkness pushing up towards the sky. Suddenly he wanted to hear the screaming rush of the ship through atmosphere, feel the kick of its shock wave pass over the dead town. He was just beginning on the road that would lead to the return of the Herculean Empire. He felt the will of his people surge through him as the ship shot through the curtain of smoke and out into a deep blue sky. The sky grew purple as he climbed, blackening into a void of bright stars. The nearby sun pulsed with anger, but could do nothing against him.

Gorgias touched the controls and the ship began to run at the sun, accelerating to a few per cent of light speed. Slowly the star grew in size, seething with the same energy he felt within himself; the star was his enemy, a watchdog that had failed to protect its planet.

When he had absorbed his fill of the star's nourishing anger, he turned it off by switching the ship into jumpspace, leaving again the universe of violent colours for the dead space of black suns.

For a long time he sat before the screen, thinking about his father's ambivalence. The grey-white backdrop of jumpspace seemed a bit different this time, suggesting strong light trying to break in from a space beyond; maybe somewhere a waterfall of light marked the frontier between the two kinds of space. He imagined the light of a universe spilling over into an abyss, a cosmos dying in one place and being born again elsewhere.

There was only one thing to do now – strike somewhere else as soon as possible, just in case there was no one left alive on Precept to report the raid.

He would need an invasion force, his father had said. Gorgias made a mental note to question Myraa again about the story of the Herculean army which had fled into the Lesser Magellanic Cloud towards the end of the war. He would have to find out if this was true or just a legend; if true, he would make an effort to contact the force, or its descendants. They might have ships and weapons that would be of use to his campaign.

Passing his hand over the panel, he summoned the star charts onto the screen and began searching for a new target.

5. THE LEGACY

'There will always be those who must
look into the dark in order to see.
– Alan McGlashan

Earth's sun settlements sparkled across the New Zealand night, a ring of habitats encircling the planet, creating the illusion of an arch standing in the ocean. Rafael Kurbi sat with Grazia on the terrace of their seaside house. The waters were swallowing the ring as the night wore on, but there was always more coming up from the other horizon as the earth turned.

Tightening his arm around Grazia, he thought, *I could drift off into death now and not mind.* Immediately the thought startled him, as once the idea of his own existence had surprised him. He relaxed. *I can live as long as I wish, but my life is precarious and could just as easily have not existed.*

'What is it, Raf?'

'Oh, nothing, just bored I suppose.'

'With me?'

He looked into her dark eyes, enjoying the paleness of her skin in starlight, and wondered how long peace and satisfaction could be endured. *Strange thought, since satisfaction must by its very nature be enough, always*, he told himself unconvincingly. Perhaps there was too much order, too much tolerance and not enough conflict.

There was plenty of disorder in the planetary colonies, increasing through the Federation corridor until one reached the dark age inside the Hercules Cluster, where almost four centuries after the war still saw the twenty worlds of the Empire cut off from earth and each other.

'Well?' Grazia asked again.

'It's not you . . .'

Three times between 2000 A.D. and 5000 A.D. the earth had destroyed itself in war, only to be rebuilt by its nearer colonies. That kind of help might never be available again. After the great war with Hercules, the colonies began to think of themselves first, while earth, untouched within its own solar system, was turning away from planet based societies. Earth was becoming a garden, slowly being enclosed by the worlds of the ring, its people slowly drifting away into the skyworlds. One day the mass of the earth and the other planets would be gone, having been used to construct the component communities of the great shell that would one day finally surround the sun, to draw the sun's energy until it was exhausted in the far future. For a time, at least, the planet would continue to belong to a humankind whose biology was relatively unchanged, to people like himself and Grazia.

I have to get back to being interested in something, he told himself, *in something other than comfort*. His friends in the surrounding communities would laugh at him when he mentioned this need for demanding work. After all, he had studied the unities of art and science, experienced the pleasures and madnesses appropriate to his five decades of life. What else did he want?

'I just feel that I should be risking something, adding to something,' he said.

'That's an old time idea, you can have it subdued.'

'But I don't want it suppressed,' he said.

She looked at him and smiled. 'That's a strange thing to say – you wouldn't know afterwards.'

'Haven't you ever wondered,' he said, 'why we haven't found any cultures different from our own, I mean really different from the humanoid patterns we know?'

'Not really.'

'Haven't you wondered why they have been only as advanced as we are, give or take a little?'

'That's just the way it is. Nothing much depends on our finding out more about it.'

'Maybe there is a superior culture out there in the galaxy – or maybe it exists only in the main group of galaxies and ours is a backwater. We haven't gone out to look for them because we're afraid. Maybe the war has made us distrust our curiosity? Maybe curiosity and ambition lead to violent conflict, I don't know. It seems wrong . . .'

'What nonsense,' Grazia said, 'it's enough that we're kind and gentle and civilized.'

'Look – we don't even use our subspace communications system to search for advanced cultures, not even in our galaxy, much less beyond. We use the system to talk to our own worlds in the corridor. Doesn't that strike you as narrow and unenterprising?'

'We mind our own business, Raf.'

'But look – we don't even know much about ourselves, what we are, what life is beyond the textbook litanies.'

'We're the form of living matter that asks foolish questions about itself,' she said. 'There are scientific people for these problems.'

'But there aren't, Grazia, you don't know how few there are.'

'Enough, I would say.'

'A few hundred. Oh, there are many technical priests who know how to run things by looking up the answers which they don't really understand. Too many areas of knowledge exist only in the computer intelligences and in old books. Very little of that lives in new human minds.'

'It's there, though.'

'But what about new work, new questions?'

'I think the artificial minds can do better,' she said.

'They only care about knowing, not doing – they have no drive, no instincts to use what they have learned. Once they know, that's enough.'

'I'm glad they know – it would be such a burden. We're made for the senses, Raf, to appreciate and experience things, not for understanding, which is an illusion anyway.'

'Then maybe those who are redesigning populations in the ring are right.'

'But they're not doing what you would want, just more so towards what I say we are. What you want was tried in Hercules, and we got warlike, unbalanced conquerors, not knowers, or appreciators.'

'How are we to evolve further?' he asked. 'We must do it by our own hand because natural selection is over.' *Maybe it's not over*, he thought, *maybe after a million years of immortality, only the most ambitious and innovative will remain.*

'I'm glad there's a place for old bodied people like ourselves,' Grazia said.

Slowly, he knew, she was going to get the better of him. But nothing she could say would rid him of the feeling that he was beginning to die, that he would continue to die no matter how often he was renewed physically, no matter how long he lived.

Julian Poincaré visited the next morning, dropping his image in from South Pole City just as Kurbi was beginning to resent the rising sun's penetration of his closed eyelids. He opened his eyes and saw the stocky man standing near the railing, looking out over the ocean.'

'Julian?'

Poincaré turned around. 'Ah, you're awake.'

'Are you here?' Kurbi asked, sitting up on the deck bed.

'Appearance only, dear friend – no substance, no reality, at least not as much as usual. You're talking to yourself.'

Kurbi looked around for Grazia, vaguely remembering that she had gotten up before dawn.

'You'll be surprised to learn,' Poincaré said, 'that our intelligence at the Pole has just had news that a Herculean Whisper Ship has wiped out the rim colony on Precept.'

'It must be Gorgias again,' Kurbi said. He stretched his long legs and stood up. 'Precept? That's in the open end of the corridor, north?'

'That's right – but why should it be Gorgias? He may be dead – we haven't heard anything for more than a century. Why can't it be someone else?'

'I think he's been in stasis. There's some evidence of previous appearances and disappearances, with decades in between. If I'm right, then they have stasis capability; that mean I'm right about there being a base, there would have to be to support the technology and the ship.'

'And you still think he's not alone?'

'I think,' Kurbi said, 'that Gorgias may have a son, daughter, even brothers or relations with him.' He started to pace back and forth on the terrace. 'A base could support quite a few people.'

'You're the expert on the Herculeans,' Poincaré said.

'The corps will have something to do.'

'And you too.'

'What are your thoughts about this?' Kurbi asked.

'I'm worried where the ship will turn up next. I think it will be soon.'

'I think so too,' Kurbi said. He felt wide awake suddenly.

'As ranking intelligence officer, I'm issuing warnings – we can expect more violence.'

'As long as it's out in the colonies, I don't think anyone in Chambers will care,' Kurbi said.

'I'll try to throw a scare into them. I want ships and resources, and I want you. If they think the ship will pose a threat to close-in worlds, they'll give me what I want.'

'Me?' Kurbi asked. He had never thought of his interest in Herculeans as resulting in any practical action. The mystery of Herculean psychology had fascinated him. He had even dreamed of time travel back into the war, just to soak up the atmosphere of those times, feel the pressure of purpose and necessity; now here was a chance to confront a living Herculean from those times.

'Julian!' Grazia said as she came out of the house. The screen came on over the terrace, darkening the sky and rising sun. She came and sat down on the deck bed.

'How are you, Grazia?'

'Fine – now tell me what you want Raf for.'

'It's up to Raf.' Poincaré shrugged and Kurbi saw another tame wolf, like himself, among the sheep of earth.

'Is there any doubt that it was a Whisper Ship?' he asked.

'Even Precept's simple computer slaves identified it. There's no doubt, Raf.'

Grazia was looking at him, her eyes saying, *Why bother, what can it matter, my love?*

'You want to go,' she said, 'you want to stir up your sense of mission, destroy your equilibrium. Over what? An old war and a madman or two. Go ahead. I couldn't care less.'

'Many people have died, Grazia,' Kurbi said.

'You wouldn't go for that alone.'

'I haven't decided yet, we're just talking.'

'What if our homes were threatened,' Pointcaré said, '– this house, what if that ship appeared in that beautiful morning sky? What if that ocean were being beamed into steam right now?'

'I'd rather not live in such a world,' Grazia said, 'the sooner they killed me the better.'

'You don't mean that,' Kurbi said. He took a step towards her, intending to sit down and hold her hand.

'Stop right there,' she said. 'Look at the two of you. You're both hoping that terrible things will happen. You may be bored with your lives, but I find ennui and changelessness quite pleasant.'

'Look at it this way,' Kurbi said, 'all we know about the Hercules-Federation War is that we fought an implacable enemy. It's just one big enigma – no records or witnesses left, at least nothing that makes for good evidence. Here's a chance to confront an individual or individuals who still have the war mentality. They remember things and they may have records.'

'We have people from then also.'

'They've mostly erased their experiences, you know that.'

'Well, there are Herculeans living on various worlds.'

'Those survivors will never open up – they've changed.'

'The simple fact of the matter,' Poincaré said, 'is quite clear and needs no justification – a Whisper Ship is a good sized nuisance. It could kill more Federation citizens, it could destroy a planet under certain conditions – Earth for example. Whatever Raf's interest, he would be useful in the hunt.'

'You're just trying to scare me, Julian,' Grazia said.

'I'm certainly not.'

'Well, it is frightening, no matter what your motive.'

'Raf, she's picking on me. Grazia, it could happen, what I say.'

Grazia laughed and lay back on the cot.

The war left us a legacy, Kurbi thought, *one which must be taken up, examined, understood; to do so is a form of loyalty to the past and truthfulness to the future.*

'Good day,' Julian said and disappeared.

Kurbi looked through the space where the man's image had stood. The ocean beyond was alive with sunlight and small sailboats. He wondered what they were thinking inside the Herculean ship countless parsecs away.

'I'm going for a swim,' Grazia said behind him.

6. TARGET

'The savage mind deepens its knowledge with the help of *imagines mundi*.'
– Claude Lévi-Strauss

'Who is the man walking in the Way?
An eye glaring in the skull.'
– Seccho

His son was shaking him awake.

'We're not coming out – the ship won't come out of jumpspace!'

He opened his eyes and understood suddenly.

'I can't tell what's wrong,' his son was saying, 'I've tried everything.'

'It's not the ship,' the Herculean said, 'this sometimes happens . . .' He got up and followed his son forwards through the ship.

The screen was blinking when they entered the control room, as if a storm were raging outside.

'Look,' his son said, 'the star analogs – they look solid now!' In normal passage, the black places marking the positions of stars in normal space were not solid objects in relation to the ship; directly ahead of them now was a giant black sphere, its surface shiny and reflective. The ship was rushing towards it at an unknown velocity.

'I've tried to alter our course half a dozen times,' his son said, 'but the ship fixes on another sphere and runs towards it.'

'We're not in the usual otherspace, but in a nearby parallel space. A quantum uncertainty within the ship's vibrancy matrix generator causes this sort of thing. I was warned against it. It doesn't happen very often, but it can't be helped. The old builders didn't have time to iron out the problem, and they were not sure it could even be solved without altering the fundamental laws of nature.'

'But you know how to get us out?'

'I'll try.'

The object ahead was now twice as large. In a few moments it covered the viewscreen. A reflection of the ship appeared in the black surface, a silver image rushing up to meet them head on. Frozen energy, the old Herculean thought, everything that a living sun is not. The continuum flickered again, leaving a slow fading flash in the black below. Suddenly the ship's image seemed to pass into them and the vessel was flitting across a stygian plain. A mock sunrise flashed on the horizon as the continuum flickered again. *Maybe we'll die*, the older Gorgias thought. He would not have to face his son, or watch him carry out his plans.

The ghastly flickering became more frequent. The Herculean passed his hand over the glowing programme plate, enjoining it to carry out its orders.

The ship switched. For a moment it seemed that a more familiar jumpspace was coming into view on the screen; then the alien space flickered again and he knew that the ship had only changed position within it.

'Tell me the truth – we may never come out.'

'You may be right, son.'

'Try again.'

'Here we go.'

The ship switched, straining to surface into the

known universe, again without success. The ship was running at another black sphere.

'What now?' his son asked. There was a trace of anger in his tone.

'Wait – try again, as often as it takes to bring us out. The uncertainty in the generator fields can't last forever by their very nature.'

'Regular watches?'

'Try three times during each watch.'

'I'll wait until you try once more,' his son said, 'then I'll get some rest and leave you to it.'

'Here we go.'

The ship switched for the third time.

The screen went black.

'Now what?' his son asked.

'I don't know . . .'

The ship's lights flickered.

'It's as if we're not getting enough power,' his son said. 'Can we check anything in here?'

'No, the receiving accumulators are a sealed mechanism.'

'You mean we get power from somewhere else?' his son asked.

'We've never taken on fuel, if you've noticed. For what this ship can do, it could never carry enough power or generate its own. I think we get it from the cluster, but I don't know how. Engineering and armouring was not my strong suit. I was just an attack force captain.'

'But if the ship works, then the power source was never destroyed!' his son said.

'We're far out of our spaces – that's probably interfering with power reception.'

All signs of movement were absent from the black screen; reality had solidified, freezing all motion.

The screen lightened, growing brighter, as if some titanic explosion were taking place outside. The ship was suddenly in a white space, and the stars, if they were stars, appeared as small black points.

The Herculean passed his hand over the panel for the fourth time and the ship switched.

The known universe recreated itself on the screen.

'We don't seem to be far from where we started,' his son said, 'maybe a dozen light years from Precept.'

Where hundreds lay dead in the dust. What did they know of the war? What had they ever done to his son? I should have tried to stop it.

But his doubts and tender feelings of mercy would not restore the Empire's power, that much was certain. His son would never accept the Empire's permanent demise; restoration was for him the one supremely valued end, overriding all conventional norms; to revive Hercules was the only way of life for him, even if in the end it might mean the death of all surviving Herculeans, including himself.

The interstellar liner drifted slowly on the screen; only minutes out of Sagan IV, it was readying to switch over into jumpspace. The Whisper Ship's beam reached out to the cylindrical hull and began pumping energy into the forward drive mass. A hole opened like a blooming flower. Gas began to spill out. The beam shifted to the mid-section and another wound opened; red light and human shapes spilled out into space.

It's the only way.

His father had left the cabin a few moments before the attack. *The whole point is to do cruel and terrible things.* Silently the beam shifted and cut its third hole.

A million miles behind the rupturing vessel, the disc of Sagan IV swam in half phase. In a few minutes port tugs would be rushing out to the dying liner. He could even expect a military ship or two, but they would be too late to threaten him.

There would be little for the rescuers to save. The ship would explode at any moment, as the laser's torrent of energy penetrated into vital areas. Was it true, he wondered, that power from the stars of home was finding its way into the Whisper Ship? He felt pride in the idea; Hercules was still a cluster of war stars, despite his father's weakness, despite Myraa's indifference.

The liner blossomed in space. Its hull flew apart as if driven by the magma of an exploding planet. The debris expanded, a small universe of mangled life, molten metal and hot plasma; bits and pieces would continue in all directions – into the local sun, into deep space, moving until all time ran out.

Suddenly, the magnification on his screen went up, revealing military vessels coming out from the orbital docks around Sagan IV, two near-planet defence cruisers summoned by the dying liner. Gorgias wondered if there was fear aboard the Federation ships as they examined the Herculean design on their screens. What were they thinking as they stared at the Whisper Ship, a legendary shape far out of its time?

They were coming fast now, growing in size until the screen switched to normal and they were plainly visible as bright stars no more than a few hundred kilometres away.

Automatically, the Whisper Ship began to pull away, shrinking Sagan IV to a blue point. The ship switched, blackening the stars and affixing them to a backdrop of desolate grey. The pursuers were gone, two stars crushed out of existence.

Gorgias waited for two black dots to appear in the

warp. A minute went by, two minutes; after five minutes there was still no pursuit.

'Are we running?'

He turned around and saw his father standing in the centre of the cabin. Fear and sadness crowded into the older man's face, constricting his muscles as if he had been crying. The old Herculean was a disgrace to his traditions.

'The liner is destroyed, and we've lost the hunters.'

His father closed his eyes. 'Where are we going now?'

'I want Myraa and the others to know before we return to base.'

'Why? Of course – it will impress them, you think.'

'It will inspire the others, perhaps, and she can't help but be affected.'

'Don't you see – it's your way of stealing courage.'

'I don't see that at all.'

His father walked up to him and struck him across the face with the back of his hand.

'You have no right to do that!'

The old Herculean struck him again and the blow threw him back in the chair. 'I'm going to beat you until you can't walk, until I can lock you up like a beast and not care.'

'Coward,' Gorgias said as he rubbed his face.

His father lunged at him and seized his throat. Gorgias felt powerful hands close on his windpipe and squeeze.

With great effort, Gorgias lifted his father by the waist and they both fell to the floor, older man on the bottom. The angry hands relaxed their hold on his throat and Gorgias struggled onto his feet.

He turned and looked at the screen. Two black dots had appeared.

'Look – hunters! I can't bother with you now. Go back to your cabin.'

He sat down at the station, passed his hand over the programme plate and rekindled the known universe for a few seconds, quenched it again, then searched for the sign of the pursuers.

The continuum was clear, but he knew that they would reappear in a few moments; the ship was leaving too clear a trail. He would have to do something to hide it quickly.

He turned around to face his father again, but the Herculean was gone.

7. AWAKENING

> 'Not till we are lost . . . do we begin to understand ourselves.'
>
> – Henry David Thoreau

'The frontier settlement on Precept,' Poincaré was saying, 'then the liner on the Sagan IV run. That's more than twenty thousand dead, Raf.'

They sat on the sun-filled terrace, breakfast before them. Grazia was sail planing over the ocean, a small white bird in a perfectly clear blue sky.

'They've dropped it in my lap,' Poincaré said, 'what do you think we should do?'

'Ask our military antiquarians.'

'I'm one of them – so are you to a degree.'

'Well?'

'I say go after the ship with a small force, hunt him down, keep a larger force on call to come running when we've found him.'

'What's your problem then?' Kurbi asked.

'I want you with me, I thought that much was obvious. Raf, you have a feel for Herculean civilization. I don't want this to be a completion of genocide. I think you can help me save whatever may be worth saving.'

'I'd say that was a charitable way of thinking about it, considering all the carnage the Herculean has caused. Do you have a choice?'

'If possible,' Poincaré said, 'I want the Whisper Ship

and its occupants captured alive. Everyone I know feels the same. They're not altruists or historians or bleeding heart Chards – they're curious, somewhat greedy men, who want the ship and its base, just to see what's there. I wouldn't mind playing with a few Herculean war toys myself.' Poincaré took a deep breath. 'Besides, it's great entertainment to think of capturing these rogues. We'll exhibit them, question them, try them, inter them for life.'

'The enemy's face is fascinating,' Kurbi said, 'especially when he is in short supply. You want me to go out and find Gorgias?'

'You still want to, don't you?'

'There's Grazia to consider – it would be dangerous. I would be giving up a life of travel and reflection.'

'There'd be travel, and you can test what you've been reflecting about. You would also be helping to save lives.'

Kurbi shrugged. 'Does that mean so much, Julian, with so many dying by choice?'

'The ones who died made no choice.'

'Life seems to be most precious when threatened. Take danger away and a whole starry civilization goes to sleep.'

'Exactly,' Poincaré said, '– you and I know that we need all the waking up we can get. This terrorist might be doing us a favour.'

'I don't think he would appreciate your view of him.'

'Now you're sounding like Grazia.'

'I sometimes wonder if I know what I want,' Kurbi said. 'Life seems to possess a fundamental flaw, especially if you know it can be prolonged indefinitely.'

'What flaw is that?'

'An inability to provide lasting satisfaction.' He looked out across the bright morning and saw Grazia's glider come sweeping in from the ocean. In a minute or two she would pass over the house. Suddenly the craft dropped below the seaside cliffs and he could not see it. The updraft would hurl it skyward again, and she would hurtle in over the house as she had done so many times before.

Kurbi picked up the half finished glass of grape juice and finished it. 'Won't you have something with me, since you're here in the flesh?'

'No thanks. Well, what do you say?'

'I don't know right now, Julian, let me think about it.'

'I won't try and sugar coat it – we may both get killed.'

'I'm well aware of that,' Kurbi said. He got up. The glider was not coming up into view.

'What's wrong?'

'The glider has not come up over the cliffs.'

Poincaré got up also and they went to the terrace steps that led down to the path. In a moment Kurbi was running across the grass to the cliff's edge a quarter of a kilometre away. Poincaré caught up with him just in time to steady him at the edge.

'There,' Julian said pointing.

The glider was in the water, one wing broken.

'She took this updraft so many times . . .'

'Let's get down there, Julian said, 'better still, I'll go down and you call the medics.'

Kurbi turned and walked quickly up to the house, feeling that his body was not his own.

'Hurry!' Julian called after him.

She had fallen to the rocks after hitting the cliff; the sea had battered her body until she was beyond repair. There was no possibility of freezing the remains or of restarting the body's regenerative systems; only cloning remained and he had rejected the idea. The person who would have come to him bearing Grazia's appearance and genetic structure would not have been Grazia, only her twin sister. For many others that would have been enough, but for him it would have been a mockery of his love for her.

He sat alone in the darkened living room and tried to choke his grief, compress it to a point and squeeze that point out of reality. Outside, the sky blazed, hurling spears of starlight through the clear wall between the living room and terrace. The glider sank in his mind and he reached out with invisible hands to stop it from hitting the cliff. She had been falling as he had talked with Julian, and he had known it; she might even have been conscious after hitting the sea rocks.

It would have been better, he thought, if she had been on the interstellar liner. That would have made more sense; better the explosive decompression of the void than the bloodying rocks; better murder than mindless chance. Anything was preferable to being reminded of frailty and the indifference of physical reality; the intended act was always superior to the unintended event.

Stupid thoughts, he told himself. Maybe he should go and help Poincaré trap his gadfly; maybe it would help him forget. It would be almost . . . as if he were searching for Grazia again.

He got up and went out on the terrace. The sky made him feel small. For a moment he felt that he understood the feelings of the outworlders, for whom life was joined to strenuous effort; out there living was valuable and dying meaningful. There they would laugh at the manner of Grazia's death; there life was stretched between demanding limits and did not try to be more;

there life spent itself so completely that little regret was possible at its end.

He thought of his son Rik, who had not come to Grazia's funeral service, and who had refused to talk with him or share his sorrow. It would do no good to search for him among the diverse worlds of the ring; he would not recognize his son if he saw him.

Rik had never reconciled himself to the fact that he had been born of natural parents and in a fairly ancient way, while all his peers in the sun settlements were creative composites drawn from genetic bank materials. Kurbi blamed himself for letting the boy leave the earth at an early age; in the ring he had come under the overwhelming influence of a myriad styles. The earth could never be the same for him again.

In a way Rik was right; only a small portion of humanity lived on earth; an even smaller portion lived the older life, which accepted leisure but little biological alteration. Perhaps, as Rik believed, the acceptance of the unmodified human form limited one's range of experiences and exercise of creative powers; while the newer, variegated humanity, Rik claimed, had overcome the old discontents.

Suddenly Kurbi was sure that he would join Poincaré, but the feeling passed; what he really wanted to do, he admitted, was to wander away from the solar system and explore the worlds of the Federation corridor. He wanted to see how people lived, and if they were happier. Julian could do without him for a time.

Grazia, he said silently. The ring of worlds in the sky blurred into a band of light as tears filled his eyes; while another part of him cursed the fact of human dependency and the insufficiency of all things.

8. HOME

> 'As to what happened next . . . when men are desperate no one can stand up to them.'
>
> – Xenophon

The stillness in the control cabin was oppressive. The ship's motion through the grey vastness seemed to be an imprisonment within a static medium. That the ship was moving was something he *knew*; but his body felt only confinement.

His father came in and stood behind him. 'Where are we going now?' he asked.

'We've lost the pursuers, but I don't want to lead them back to the base if I'm wrong. We're going back to Myraa – later we'll go to the base to pick up some equipment I want.'

'What do you have in mind?' His father's tone was almost friendly, as if he were another person.

'What do you care?'

'I'm sorry I can't feel the way you do. Can you feel how sorry I am?'

'How can you bring yourself to care about the deaths of our enemies?'

'I can't help it – it's been so long, what can those alive now know of the old struggle?'

'I'm going to leave you at the base – unless you still want to help.'

'If something happens to you, I will never be able to leave the base. Leave me with Myraa instead.' His father's voice was almost a whisper. *He's inside me*, Gorgias thought, *I'll never get rid of him*. 'I think I might like living with Myraa and the others.' *Punish him, don't give him what he wants.*

'I've changed my mind – we'll go back to the base first. I'll need you to help me load and handle two or three gravitic units. You do know something about them, don't you?'

'Yes, very well,' his father said, 'but later you must leave me on Myraa. It's what I want now.'

Gorgias turned around in his station chair.

'Must – there is little that I must do. I'll see.' The old Herculean was trying to manipulate him now.

'Thank you,' his father said.

He wants to get away from me, forget I ever existed. What would it take to convince him I am right? I would have to destroy our enemies completely, until not a single stone could rise up against me.

'I'll stay in the aft cabin,' his father said and left the control area.

As he watched the bulkhead door slide shut, a sudden fear gripped Gorgias, as if he had been cut off from everything real. The past was shrinking away from him, leaving him alone and naked before a stone wall of infinite height and thickness, a structure that he would never be able to penetrate. He could not imagine what lay on the other side, but he knew that he desired it above everything else. He turned back to the screen and closed his eyes to shut out the timelessness of jump-space; visualizing the wall before him, he made an effort to pierce its substance. His eyes came up against a fine texture of sandy pits and scars, where a nameless weathering had worked to breach the stone . . .

He opened his eyes, suddenly aware that he had been dozing. The screen was filled with the grey-white light of the continuum, casting its pallor into the cabin. He looked at his hands. The skin seemed dead and dry, as if the flesh were about to fall away from the bones. *Everything in jumpspace is dead; everything that passes through dies a little.* He rubbed his hands together and they fell away from his arms . . .

He sat up and realized that he had been dreaming about being awake. The screen was a normal grey with black stars; passage home was a quarter over and there was no sign of hunters.

He got up and paced the cabin, dreaming of the new sortie.

As the universe reappeared on the screen, the Hercules Cluster took up half the field of view ahead, a globe of fireflies exploding out from a centre of concentrated light. Within a half hour the cluster became the entire universe as the ship penetrated towards the base star inside.

Within another hour the concealing cloud was behind the ship and the dead world of the base floated on the screen. The ship brought itself in low over the scarred surface and drifted into the receiving tunnel through the sequence of locks, sliding finally into its familiar berth.

Home, young Gorgias thought bitterly, *all there is of it.*

Once, the core of the Empire had consisted of twenty worlds, all dead now. He still remembered the roll taught to him by his father. New Anatolia, Capital of the Empire; Gorgias, home of the Empire's creators; Vis and Sivat, worlds of the mental arts; Lash and Bram, planets for soldiers; Indra, the water world; Avat and Rishna, where armourers built the instrumentalities of war; Rud and Panis, shipbuilding planets, where a few inspired designers, together with a team of fleeing armourers had built the two known Whisper Ships; Nahus and Ush, places for the arts and architecture; Ganesa, a world for poets and songsingers; Manus, a world for historians and computer libraries; Yama, the wilderness where young soldiers went to test themselves; Jas, Ulys and Mizon, outer worlds for astronomers, physicists and scientific researchers of every kind. All this within a space of 50 light years. The cluster's diameter of 100 light years contained 10,000 times as many stars as any equal volume of space. Here was room to grow, to concentrate creative energies, to create the greatest civilization in the galaxy; no wonder the cluster had earned the Federation's envy; but here the Herculean Empire would come to be again.

He got up from the station and went aft to the side lock, which was already open. He stepped out into the stillness and looked around. The lights were still on around the stony berth. The metal door leading out from the chamber of six berths was still open. Suddenly he felt love for the base; it was strong and constant; self-maintaining, it would last forever.

His father came out and stood beside him. 'What will you need me for?' he asked.

'I'll need you to help me load two gravitic units and a tug-scooter.'

'Right now?'

'Yes – that's all I came for.'

Gorgias led the way from the berth, through the metal door and down the long corridor into the war room, around the table to another door. Pulling it open, they went through and followed a downward sloping passage which led into a supply warehouse composed of a hundred interlocking chambers. There were a dozen levels below this area; the lowest floor housed the life support devices, which were powered by the thermal energy of the planet's core. As long as this world remained warm inside and the homeostatic slave intelligences continued to channel energy to the various systems, the base would live, its synthesizers producing air and foodstuffs, more than he would ever need. The berth would stock the ship with sufficient synthesizer mass and make subtle adjustments and repairs in the sealed sub-molar systems that received the energy to run the drive. At times it disturbed him to know that he understood so little of the ship or the base's workings, but the great builders and armourers were gone and there was no one to teach him. Where, for example, was the power source for the Whisper Ship? Somewhere in the cluster, but where? Where was the other ship, if there was one? Given enough time, he might come to understand more of what the base contained; but only the growth of a new population of Herculeans would be capable of retrieving the legacy of the past, bringing all the skills and knowledge out of the records and technical examples back into the container of living individuals, who could then shape new developments.

'Where would the grav units be?' Gorgias asked.

'In the wall closets,' his father said, 'most were never unpacked.'

The lights in the room were dim. The greenish walls rose to a height of ten feet and met a grey ceiling. The air was cool and odourless. 'I was here when the base was opened,' the old Herculean said, 'when they were bringing in all the supplies still stored here.' He went ahead to the far wall and slid open a large closet door, revealing case after case containing work scooters and gravitic workhorses, each packed in a clear plastic block.

Gorgias went up to the open closet and peered in at

the tools. The scooter had seats for two, hover and propulsive controls that seemed obvious, and a small rack in the back; the gravitic units were featureless solid rectangles about a metre long and half a metre tall, with attachment fingers located at each right angle. On-off pressure plates were yellow and stood out from the dark green of the unit; whether the device would be used to push, pull, or lift depended on the position in which it would be attached.

'How much can these handle?' Gorgias asked.

'I don't know the practical limit,' his father said, 'though I suspect that they could not push a planet. Anything substantially smaller, depending on where it is, on a planetary surface or in free fall, would be fair game, I suppose.'

His father seemed calmer, as if their violent confrontation had purged him of his fears and doubts. Maybe he would become his old self again and be of use after all.

'Can we use the scooter to ferry the units to the ship?'

'I think so,' his father said.

'Let's unpack then.'

Together they pulled the scooter from its niche onto the floor. The plastic block was soft and gelatinous to the touch and came off easily. Gorgias peeled off the covering on the grav units and stacked them on the back of the scooter. He sat in the front saddle and his father got on in back.

'Here we go.'

Gorgias pressed down on the hover control plate gently and the scooter lifted from the floor; he pressed on the propulsion plate and the scooter moved forwards. Grasping the stick, he steered the machine towards one of the marked service doors, which slid open to reveal a direct tunnel connecting to the berth area.

As the scooter carried them through the passageway, he thought of all the weapons stored in the warehouse, rooms and rooms of shelves, closets and cubbyholes turned away from the stars of home, filled with more military hardware than he could name; enough armaments to equip ten divisions.

Another door slid open and let them out into the berth chamber. Gorgias steered the scooter alongside the ship and into the open lock, stopping just past the inner door.

'We can leave it here, near the bulkhead,' he said and got off.

'What will you use the units for?' his father asked as he dismounted.

A suspicion grew in Gorgias's mind, the result of the question as well as the older man's change in approach. Was he planning to act against him? The only way to find out was to tell him what he wanted to know and watch his reaction.

'Come with me and find out.'

'Then you don't want to leave me here?'

'Tell me, why did you give me the ship if you were so worried about how I would use it?'

The Herculean did not answer immediately. 'It must be because a part of me still thinks as you do. Once all of me felt the way you do – I taught you to do so. There seemed to be no other way to live and act in the periods between stasis, especially when we thought one of our armies had escaped and might return. So much was promised by the armourers towards the end of the war – we all thought those weapons could make a difference.'

'They would have, if there had been time to build them.'

'I think,' his father said, 'that I would like to live on Myraa's World. Leave me there, forget me and do as you wish, but don't leave me here . . .'

'Very well.' It would be better to agree with him now, and see what happened later. He suspected that the older man was physically ill in some way, and his mind might be affected. But what doctor from the Federation knew enough to treat a Herculean? Completely homeostatic, requiring no medical care except in serious accident cases, the race had been designed for endurance; in terms of the need for rest, recovery from infection and general vitality, a Herculean could outperform a traditional earthborn by a factor of three to five.

'Thank you,' his father said.

Historically, Earth citizens had been shy of biological engineering, fearing the loss of versatility to specialization if the practice got out of hand; but as the Federation grew, pockets of humankind diverged from one another, culturally and biologically, until the first settlements in the Hercules Cluster reached out for a truly improved human type, creating the long-lived Herculeans. Few were left now, he thought sadly, himself and his father and the handful on Myraa's World. He had not heard of any others. Genocide had been all but complete; but in failing to be complete, the earthborn had made a fatal error, one which he would live to see them regret. They could demoralize his father and Myraa's survivors, but they would never cow him.

'Let's get going,' he said to his father.

Turning from the open lock, he led the way into the control room. He sat down in the station chair and waited for the lock to close. His father came and stood at his right.

'Well, what are you plans?' There was an almost lighthearted tone in the older man's voice.

Gorgias touched the map retrieval plate and the screen lit up, revealing a solar system of twelve planets. 'Here, six hundred light years from earth, lies New Mars, fourth planet from the twin suns. The various settlements have more than 20 million people. The planet has no heavy defences, and no reason to expect us . . .'

'What's your idea?'

'I'm going to destroy most of the life on the planet,' Gorgias said.

9. THE RING

> 'One must somehow find a way of loving the world without trusting it; somehow one must love the world without being worldly.'
>
> – G.K. Chesterton

> '. . . the love of a man for a woman is like an attempt at transmigration, at going beyond ourselves, it inspires migratory tendencies in us.
>
> – Ortega y Gasset

He was alone, going where he wished, and the fact made him feel guilty.

As he stood looking out the window of his resort room, Rafael Kurbi realized that he did not know where he was going. The green mountainside was peaceful outside his window. Here in the sun settlements of earth's ring, a quarter of a million worlds, each a different environment and subculture, beckoned with the promise of novelty and human contact; he could change worlds as he would clothing.

From inside, the ring was a cloud of glittering insects, rivalling the stars in brightness, a milky way of human living spaces cutting across the galactic background; at the centre was Earth, oasis of origins, a place to be looked at, admired, even worshipped, but not lived on. People found it strange that he had cared to dwell there so long; even though a large population shared his preference, it was a tiny minority compared to the population of the ring.

The North American mountain landscape outside his window – peaks and fir trees, outcroppings and boulders – was all perfectly safe and accurate. The weather could be varied to taste, streams stocked with perfect fish, woods filled with replaceable game, the air filled with birds. If only he could order a glider with Grazia in it.

He was standing with his head towards the centre of the small world; across a space of air he could see houses and roadways attached to the opposite surface fifty kilometres away. Sunlight shafted down the centre of the egg shaped air space, reflected in by a large mirror at one end of the environment; sunpower also ran the recycling plant located on the outside at the other end of the worldlet.

Less than twenty kilometres away in space hung another world, one filled with water, where visitor's hotels provided a view of aquatic human life; there one could swim to a sun window and look out at the stars.

Pulling aside the slide window, Kurbi stepped out on the terrace and took a deep breath. The air was cool and clean and stimulating. Standing there, he felt little of the stress and anguish that he knew were inside him, readying to take over.

'How are you feeling?' a familiar voice asked from behind.

He turned and said, 'Hello, Julian – are you here?'

The image shook its head. 'Waste of time – just dropped in to see if you'd changed your mind.'

'No. Any more news of the Herculean ship?'

'Nothing at all.'

'Maybe that's the end of it.'

'I don't think so. I've been doing some checking – this ship has appeared before. From the scattered Herculeans still alive on more than a dozen star systems, besides those on Myraa's World, I've learned that the Whisper Ship is probably manned by an officer named Gorgias and his son of the same name. He's more than four centuries old, his son at least half that age – but much of that time may have been spent in stasis somewhere . . .'

Like an old disease virus, Kurbi thought, *or a spore*.

'There must be an undiscovered base,' Julian said. 'If there is not, then the ship may very well disappear for lack of supplies and repair facilities. We were never able to capture a Whisper Ship – the only record is of one destroying itself rather than surrender. Some of the Herculean legend reported to me says that the ship is tied to the personality of its commanding officer in some way, and destroys itself when the officer dies. In any case, this vessel has appeared in centuries past, each time taking action against some locale in the Federation, always disappearing for long stretches of time.'

'What's the point, then?'

'Revenge, from what I've managed to guess. A few of the Herculeans questioned by our operatives have shown admiration for what has happened. A thing like this could grow.'

'Into what?'

'Insurrection – takeover of a world here and there.'

'What do we care?'

'There is civil order to preserve – and some of the Chamber members won't stand for a Herculean survivor causing trouble. They'll do anything to quash it, out of pride.'

'Let the locals do it – they do most everything else for themselves.'

'Raf, what it comes down to is this – we want the ship and we want the base. It's a combination of curiosity, murder, and general unfinished business. There may be more attacks on transports, and many worlds have no protection against attack from space – they have no need of it, since it's not the kind of thing that happens very often.'

'You can do well without me, Julian. Look at the worlds around earth – what do they care about anything that happens to old style human types like you and me and the frontier worlds? Reality is a menu they write each morning; their bodies are clay to be moulded from one generation to the next. The acts of this terrorist are part of an unpleasant game for them, one they don't care for much, so they give it to you or me. You know, Julian, these Herculeans are probably a lot like you and me, relics from another time; and they're out there kicking and screaming, getting in their licks before they're blown away.'

'That's very nice, Raf, but they could destroy the earth, the ring, most of the life in the solar system, if they can get followers. They're probably not aware of that yet, but they'll catch on. It's up to those of us who have an idea of the potential danger to stop them.'

Kurbi did not reply.

'It's that serious, Raf.'

'You think they may have the equipment to do that?'

'If they have a base, maybe worse. They may not be aware of what they have. We don't have much will to fight back. The Whisper Ship could do quite a bit of damage if it came into our sun space. How do you protect the ring? It wasn't made to be defensible.'

'You're assuming a lot of motivation, a lot of hatred on their part.'

'Raf, you know more than I do how we destroyed their entire culture – twenty worlds razed to the ground!' He paused for a moment. 'It's possible none of this may happen, we may never hear of the ship again – its range is not limited and Gorgias may simply go off somewhere into the galaxy and live quietly. I don't know – but I do have a job to do as intelligence officer, and I do have some pride in how well I do it. You're a Herculean expert. It's my duty to recruit you.'

'I wouldn't be much good to you now, Julian. The answer is still no.'

Abruptly, Poincaré was gone. Kurbi was alone again with the perfect view, a cool breeze and the weight of a loss that could never be made good. *What in all eternity do I want*, he asked himself, knowing full well that it was involvement, a context in which he was needed. Poincaré was offering that, but it was not enough because Kurbi would not let it be enough out of stubbornness. *Maybe there comes a time when having lived for a time is enough, and further life is useless unless one becomes a different person. The person I am must die*, he told himself, but he was not sure there would ever be a successor.

On the world devoted to physical pleasures he paid to fall in love. The fee was his permission to record his memory and the time limit was three weeks; but the completeness of the illusion convinced him that more than a year had passed.

She was beautiful, brown haired and brown eyed, buxom and heavy hipped – an old style human type from before the changes; of course, she was tailor made, to be mindwiped after his term of involvement, but he knew that only later. When she was with him, he forgot the past and believed completely. She spoke perfectly, smiled appealingly – perhaps she even understood what he said to her during those long nights when the moon never set. She was a professional, who somewhere had her own life and would return to it. In the end she helped destroy his sense of the unique, which he had gained so painfully, so completely with Grazia.

I need something constructive to do, he told himself. Julian's offer intrigued him, but he felt that he would be of no use in his present state. He wondered if he were afraid of the danger, of dying. What would it be like to confront a Herculean who had only one desire – to kill those who had destroyed his world. *My past is as dead as theirs*. Again he found himself sympathizing with the Herculeans.

I want to live after all, he concluded.

On the dream world he found, and lost, Grazia three times.

One hundred kilometres long, the asteroid had been motorized and brought in from the outer solar system more than a thousand years ago. It had been bored, hollowed and honeycombed in thousands of places, creating chambers of safety for the dreamers, who lived an endless succession of dream sequences. This subculture believed in the biological history of the body and old brain – letting that history of layered impulses, instincts and images bubble to the surface of their dream lives in violent, often cruel fantasies –

– Grazia came to him in his tomb, opened the sleep crypt and asked him why he was fleeing from all that was alive. She took his hand and together they were borne up through a long tunnel, emerging at last in a sunny landscape of trees and gentle hills.

The earth smelled of flowers and earth. Here a stiff winged black bird swooped towards them, seized

Grazia by the torso and nearly cut her in two, carrying the remains off into the blue, cloudless sky –

TRY AGAIN.

– They waited in a garden, she looking up at the sky from time to time, where the hot sun rode. Slowly its light increased, suffusing the entire sky, until the nova's heat blew away the planet's atmosphere, melting the flesh from their bodies, leaving for an instant two skeletons embracing –

AND AGAIN.

– He had come back in time to run towards the cliff edge. High over the sea, Grazia's glider was dropping towards the wall face, gaining speed as it approached the air currents near the shore. He stopped at the edge and started to wave her off, but the craft continued its approach until the sudden downdraft tumbled it out of control, smashing it up against the wall, sending it finally to the rocks and breakers below. Giant crabs scurried out of the surface as the ocean retreated, and he watched them pry the body out of the cockpit and pick it clean, leaving the skeleton to bleach in the sun –

TRY AGAIN?

No, he said within himself, I'm not suited to this kind of life, I'll never be able to make it work.

WE ARE SORRY, they said and let him go.

10. NEW MARS

'The Tree of Knowledge is not that of Life.'
– Byron

Rafael Kurbi arrived on New Mars with only the clothes he was wearing and his identity disc. When the shuttle from the starship touched down at Port Deimos, the Captain told him over the intercom to stay in his cabin.

A few minutes later a man came to see him.

'Rafael Kurbi?' the man asked as the door slid shut behind him.

'Yes,' Kurbi said and got up from his bunk.

'My name is Rensch, Port Commissioner for New Mars. Why are you coming here?' The man spoke Federation, but with a harsh accent that made the words startlingly unfamiliar. He was of middle height, with closely cropped black hair, slightly grey at the temples; his hands were gnarly, thick boned. He looked at Kurbi with eyes that seemed to hide amusement, perhaps even contempt.

'To live, maybe,' Kurbi said. Suddenly he became aware of his dishevelled state. He needed clean clothes, a bath and a shave. The starship had not been a luxury vessel. *A pervert from earth*, Rensch was probably thinking.

'Why? A Federation citizen of your rank and wealth, what would you want here? Are you an intelligence operative? I don't mind, personally and officially, but I would like to know.' He ran his hand through his coarse hair and scratched the back of his head.

'What would you know about me?' Kurbi asked, immediately regretting the challenging tone of the question. 'I want to live here a while, see a little of how you live,' he added before the other could answer.

'I know that you are from Earth itself, rather than from the urban ring, that you are a relatively unmodified human type, unlike the extravagantly doctored ringers. This will make you less of a curiosity to our people. Will you make official trouble if I turn you away?'

For a moment there was silence as Kurbi looked into Rensch's face. 'Do you have that right?' Kurbi asked. 'I'm sorry Commissioner,' he added quickly, 'I shouldn't have asked that – no, I won't make any trouble for you, but I hope you will let me stay.'

Rensch considered for a moment. 'You'll have to work here,' he said, 'we don't sell much in goods or services and we don't exchange much credit with earth – we trade mostly, for what the star freighters bring a few times a year. We're mostly self-sufficient, but improvements from the Federation have helped increase our population and it's getting harder to stay that way. Many of our people feel threatened.'

'How do you mean?'

'Their way of life . . .'

'What can I work at?'

'You'll have to work for food and lodgings. You'll start here in the port, helping to unload what the shuttle brings down. When you've done, come to me and I'll see what else I can do. If I can't find much, you'll have to leave when the freighter goes.'

'I'll be working for you, then?'

'I'm your boss as long as you're in the port.'

'I hope you can help me – because I want to see more of your world. By the way, where can I stay?'

'There are a few rooms behind my office – you can stay there. Come with me now.'

Kurbi followed him out of the cabin, down the shuttle's central passageway to the open lock, where a ramp led down to the unloading dock. Rensch started down ahead of him, but Kurbi paused for a moment to look out at New Mars. The port was a vast machine of black and silver metal, squatting under a sky of low, driving clouds; a drizzly rain floated down and the air smelled of ozone.

He went down the ramp to where Rensch was waiting for him.

'This is the only port we have,' the Commissioner said loudly. 'The rest of the planet is agricultural – about 20 million people, but thinly scattered across a large land surface, three continents, all joined by passable land bridges.'

'You were born here?' Kurbi asked.

'Yes – we wouldn't stand for Federation officials here.'

Rensch turned and led the way across the slippery surface of the dock to a small building a hundred metres away. There was a hand operated glass door. Inside, his office was lit by old style flourescent tubes; the desk and chairs were wrought iron. The Commissioner crossed the room and opened a green wooden door.

Kurbi followed and looked inside.

'There's a bunk and toilet,' Rensch said.

The light in the small room was dim and there was no window, only a ventilation louvre. The toilet seemed tc be a simple flush device which used water; the bunk was long and narrow.

'It'll do,' Kurbi said.

'There's no other place I can put you right now.'

Rensch went back to his desk and sat down behind it. Kurbi followed him and sat down in one of the crude iron chairs facing the desk. The black metal was cold to the touch.

'We're not a rich planet,' Rensch said, 'as you can see. And we're not about to open to tourism.'

'These chairs are handmade?'

'Yes – why?'

'Why don't you import high energy generating plants, computers and autocybers, and cut down on human effort?'

'Mr. Kurbi,' Rensch said, '– you don't mind if I use that form of address –'

'Not at all.'

'– you see, we don't believe in life without work. I mean work that supports life, not leisure work as you would know it; we don't believe in working so well that we make ourselves obsolete . . .'

'Excuse me, Commissioner,' Kurbi said, 'but your hard accent and occasional unfamiliar words make it hard for me to follow you. Could you speak more slowly?'

'Yes – stop me when I use a local word. Yes – our history is made of the lives of people who came here after seeing what leisure had done to worlds nearer Earth. We work all our lives and our lives are filled up.'

'Do you think this way?'

'I've had contact with offworlders. To be honest, they interest me, which is why I agreed to let you stay even though you will not fit in . . .' He trailed off and was silent.

'When do I start?' Kurbi asked, trying to be cheerful.

'You'll have some machinery to help with the lifting, and a few co-workers, but be prepared for sore muscles during the first few weeks. Do you really want to do this?'

'I'll stay as long as you'll have me,' Kurbi said.

In the first two weeks he worked below the port, in the first level below the surface, where a conveyor belt brought cargo from the shuttle as well as from ocean going ships. Here he picked up crates with a small pincer truck and drove them to one of several warehouses near the edge of the port. There were a hundred workers toiling with him, each operating a truck.

Two men worked directly with him. One was a tall white haired man named Den, who was only nineteen years old, and a thin, olive skinned man with three fingers missing from his left hand. At first both men limited themselves to smiling at Kurbi; later they started to ask questions.

'Why work, offworlder?' Den asked one morning.

'I need to.'

Den shrugged.

'How did you hurt yourself?' Kurbi asked the two-fingered man.

'Machine,' he said and spat as he positioned a crate on Kurbi's pincer lifts.

'What's your name?'

'Two-fingers, what else. Two will do . . .'

Den laughed nearby.

Kurbi would look forward to driving out of the long tunnel onto the surface, where the giant iron work warehouses stood under a cloudy sky. The sun came out in his third week, a double star more white than yellow, but it warmed him in the afternoons when he grew damp from the port's cold, humid basement world.

At the end of each day he ate with Rensch in the

office. Food was brought in from the worker's kitchen by one of the cooks, usually green vegetables, a piece of meat and bread. Rensch brewed a black tea himself, which Kurbi came to depend on to get him going in the cold mornings.

The Commissioner would always be looking at him when they ate.

'I don't think my sore muscles are a novelty anymore,' Kurbi said. 'You expect something from me, don't you?' He chewed his food and waited for an answer.

'I don't think I understand you, Kurbi. Have you come here to be as far away as you can from your past life?'

'You understand me,' Kurbi said and took a sip of tea.

'Is it working?'

'I think so – I would have left.'

'May I ask . . .'

'I loved someone very much – she died.'

'That is why you came here?'

'You don't think it's enough, do you? You don't have to answer. I loved her too much, it might be said. But she should not have died, there was no reason for it, and in such a way that she could not be revived.'

'Revived?'

'There was too much brain damage for her to regain anything of herself.' Rensch seemed to be looking at him as if he were a fool.

'Isn't death frightening to you here?'

Rensch drained his tea and put the cup carefully down on his desk. 'I know enough, Mr. Kurbi, to know that you would think of us as superstitious in our view of death. No, death is a way to a greater life. We believe in a merciful God.'

Kurbi swallowed a mouthful of bread. 'I had heard – how do you manage it?'

Rensch was not offended by the scepticism of the question. 'The universe would be meaningless,' he said, 'if it were not a prelude to something else. Nature is a place of testing and achievement – even you believe in achievement, otherwise life, especially immortal life, would be pointless and empty, a vastness of stars and matter and life . . . simply existing in a mindless process.'

'You've been in space?' Kurbi finished the last piece of meat and took a sip of tea.

'Yes.' He shrugged. 'In any case, that is how most of the people here see things.'

'And you?'

'I don't know. I am sure that your worlds are not committing suicide every day – they live and achieve, that much I know.'

Outside, the rain came down in a sudden rush. Kurbi suddenly appreciated the pot of warm tea on Rensch's desk, and the indoor companionship of another who seemed to be interested in serious questions.

'I'd like to see the countryside,' Kurbi said.

'I can probably get you a vehicle – no, that's no good, you would have to abandon it when you ran out of fuel. We refine our own, but there are severe limits. Anything advanced, you see, would change us. It might be best for you to rely on your feet, you'll see more that way. Better still, ride our freight line. It's limited, but it will get you across the continent. Also, if you stick to the line, we'll know where you are. You might get stuck somewhere.'

There was a silence between them. 'What's your first name?' Kurbi asked.

'Nicolai – a few people call me Nico, usually when they want something.'

Kurbi became aware of voices outside, workers going home in the rain. He turned around in his chair and saw rubber draped shapes passing the glass door.

Turning back to Nicolai, Kurbi asked, 'Why, then, does this port exist? From what you say the industry here is not what you want.'

'True – there are those who would like to close the port down. They want to do without the conveniences we import or manufacture here. Without the rail line, our growing rural population would have no relief in time of natural disaster, or famine, or when the need for medical care arises. Happily, we are part of the Federation, so those of us with traditional ideas cannot enforce them. The port stays because too many of us need its imports and industry, whether we like it or not. The port also stands as a way into another kind of life for the young, and it will affect individuals of each generation . . .'

'It seems to affect you.'

Nicolai sighed. 'It's hard not to think of the number of worlds beyond this sky, especially when they send ships that you can see and touch. Maybe those worlds know something we don't. It's startling for me to think that on many worlds people die only when they want to. There are those here who don't believe this.'

'What is the lifespan here?'

'Very low – one hundred thirty earth years is the upper limit, but it can be as low as thirty-five in bad places.'

'And people accept this, knowing that they might live longer?'

'They do – you see they don't know anything, they only hear it's possible to live longer. I believe that people want to die, not only because they look forward to another life, but because life tires them out.' Nicolai took a deep breath. 'I can see a time when I may want to leave, Rafael.'

'In order not to die?'

'I'm not afraid of dying – I don't see what I could do with a longer life, unless I changed. I can't imagine what it would be like.' He paused and looked directly at Kurbi. 'Would it be hard, Raf?'

'To do what?'

'To live as you have lived.'

'As hard as it is for me to be here. It can be done.'

'Would you help me if I . . . changed?'

'Of course, Nico.'

The rain stopped its clatter. Kurbi got up and went to stand looking out the office window. Mists rose from the iron and concrete street and nearby walkways. Night had fallen during the rainstorm. Craning his neck to peer up at the overcast sky, Kurbi realized that he had not seen the stars in months.

11. THE ROCK

'. . . everything is permitted.'
– Dostoevsky

The exit beacon for New Mars was a black dot pulsing on and off in otherspace, sweeping the continuum in sections that covered a sphere once every hour, an interstellar lighthouse that could be seen by any ship, regardless of approach vector. The Whisper Ship came out automatically, asserting again its claim to being an object in Einsteinian Space. A billion kilometres below the ship, the twin suns of the New Mars system floated in their fiery embrace of shared plasmas and magneto-gravitic force fields.

Young Gorgias woke up only a few moments before exit, feeling empty and without the usual memory of dreams. The view on the screen shifted to a schematic of the solar system below the ship; the non-organic intelligence was searching for an asteroid of sufficient size and orbital path, according to orders.

Gorgias watched and waited. One ellipse after another appeared, both inside and outside the orbit of New Mars. As soon as a suitable object was found, the ship would move to acquire it.

Finally all the ellipses faded from the screen except one. It intersected the orbit of New Mars at less than a million kilometres from the planet, and the object orbiting the primaries in that path was nearing the intersect point rapidly. The screen showed the orbit of New Mars in green, the rock's in red. The two bodies would be at their closest approach within a day.

The schematic map faded and the stars reappeared as the ship dove towards the orbit of New Mars. The twin stars grew brighter, filling the cabin with a yellow-white light.

Gorgias heard the door slide open and shut behind him. Turning around, he saw his father standing in front of the exit.

'I'll help, if you want,' the old Herculean said.

Again, Gorgias felt suspicious. 'You're still divided within yourself.'

'I can't turn against my own kind.'

'You're just afraid I may be right. If I succeed, you want to be in on it.'

'I don't know – I don't know myself very well. I wish I could be certain like you are.'

'Loyalty to the dead, to the past confers certainty. It means being a good soldier, which you have not been for a long time.'

'I am still a soldier,' his father said. 'If I may say so, this is not a war.'

'This is a different kind of war!' Gorgias shouted. 'You still fail to understand that.'

'I hope you are right.'

'I am,' Gorgias said in a lower voice. He would have to order the older man around, make some use of him. At any rate, he would not have to worry about active opposition. 'You'll do your part as long as I command this ship and we're both alive.'

Four hours later, the screen acquired a view of the rock, three kilometres of nickel-iron, a hilly surface pitted with small craters, veined with cracks and deep crevasses, encrusted with small mountains huddling together under the silence of stars.

The ship passed over the rock and took up a forward station position, retreating before the flying mountain towards the rendezvous with New Mars.

Gorgias watched the ship's intelligence throw an abstract of the asteroid on the screen; small red dots appeared, marking the places where the gravitic units would be installed in order to change the asteroid's path.

The normal view reappeared as the ship circled the rock. Laser tongues reached out to mark the surface as well as scoop out the depressions that would receive the gravitic pushers. Its task completed, the ship returned to the forward station point.

Gorgias went aft to the sidelock and checked the scooter. He put on the light space suit and felt the cool oxygen begin to circulate over his body. Then he turned around and saw his father putting on the other suit.

'I'll give you a hand,' the older Herculean said over the intercom. 'I could handle the second unit.'

He wants to stop me, Gorgias thought.

'I can manage by myself.'

'I'll come along as a back up, in case of accident.'

'There's no time to discuss it,' Gorgias said and turned to press the lock touchplate. The inner door opened and he drifted the scooter into the chamber. They both mounted the seats as the inner door closed.

The outer door opened and Gorgias ran the scooter out from the ship; fifty metres out he turned the steering stick to the right and faced the asteroid. Ahead, the rock floated against the background of the central galactic regions.

Gorgias ran the scooter forward. The asteroid grew

larger, threatening him as it appeared for a moment to bear down from above; in a moment, it seemed, it would crush him and his father against the ship; but the illusion passed as he oriented himself with a backwards glance at the ship. He was sitting upright on the scooter; the ship was behind him, not below; the rock was by definition ahead, and down was where his feet happened to be resting.

He turned right again and passed across the shorter face of the rock, then left as he circled around to the longer face. Three quarters of the way he noticed the red glow where the rock was still hot from the laser lash.

Turning to face the rock, he pushed the scooter towards the first marker, in the upper right quadrant. The rock wall grew to cover the whole sky, and the heated area became a staring eye. His mind quickly pictured a mouth for the face, in a faint slash cutting across the lower quadrants; a central mountain straddling the quadrant corners passed for a nose. The left eye was invisible because it was closed. In a moment the illusion fell apart as the scooter came in close.

Reorienting himself again, Gorgias turned the small craft to run parallel with the surface. The rock was glowing ahead, throwing a red light out of the crater. Gorgias stopped the scooter at the rim and dismounted. Taking one of the grav units off the rear carriage, he stepped up to the depression and went over the edge, floating down slowly in the asteroid's minimal attraction.

Reaching bottom, he knelt down on the warm rock and pushed down with the unit until the attachment fingers entered the surface slightly; in a moment, he knew, the four probes would telescope into the harder rock, expanding to form a strong hold.

Turning, he jumped out of the hole with one

upwards push and landed near the scooter. His father was standing at the crater's edge, looking down.

'I didn't need you,' Gorgias said.

'I was here if you did,' his father said without turning around. He was still staring down into the hole.

'Let's go,' Gorgias said and mounted the scooter.

The figure of his father turned slowly and padded towards him, finally reclaiming its rear seat.

The scooter went straight up for a thousand metres, then Gorgias turned around and circled to the other side of the rock. New Mars floated two million kilometres away, a brown, green and blue disc slowly growing larger.

Gorgias brought the scooter down parallel with the rock's surface again, and moved towards the crater's glow just ahead, stopping a few metres from the edge. Again he got off and took the grav unit from the rear. His father sat quietly in his seat, as if reproaching him, or confirming something. *What does he want*, Gorgias asked himself, *why did he come? He can't stop me. Does he want to convince himself that I mean to do what I say?* He took the unit in both hands, walked up to the laser excavation, dropped over the edge and brought his legs into a kneeling position to drive the unit into the rock in one motion when he landed.

When the device was secure, he stood up and jumped back up to the rim.

'You did not have to come,' he said to his father as he stepped carefully up to the scooter.

'I was here if you got hurt or needed help.'

So you say, he thought. 'Let's get back,' he said as he clambered back into the front seat.

Overhead, the disc of New Mars had grown slightly larger.

In the control room Gorgias watched as the ship moved behind the asteroid, circling until the rock was between itself and New Mars. Trailing behind, the ship would be invisible to detection, if by chance scanners were looking its way.

The rock filled the screen, obscuring the growing disc of the planet. At his right the two primaries blazed in space as the ship's motion brought them into the screen's field of view.

'It's not pushing away from us,' his father said at his side, 'the gravitics may be too weak.'

You were hoping for this, Gorgias thought, *you were willing to help me because you knew this would happen.*

Gorgias whirled his chair around and stood up to face the old Herculean. 'Liar, traitor! You knew this all the time.'

'Look!' his father shouted, 'It's moving.'

Gorgias turned to see the rock pulling away from the screen. The ship had activated the gravitics, accelerating the rock into a collision orbit with New Mars; by the time it reached the planet's atmosphere, the asteroid would be moving at better than 100 kilometres per second, and would strike the surface with devastating effect.

Schematics appeared again, confirming the rock's new course. A map of the planet's Western Hemisphere showed that the point of impact would be in the ocean just off the largest port city.

A view of the receding rock appeared. It was growing smaller as the ship fell behind. The asteroid continued to shrink, until it revealed behind it the growing disc of New Mars.

12. PLANETGRAZER

'O waste of Loss, in the hot mazes, Lost
Among bright stars
On this most weary unbright cinder, Lost!'
– Wolfe

Rafael Kurbi sat in the open door of the freight car and watched the flat countryside rush by him. Once in a long while he would see a lonely house on the horizon, its smoke a thin wire joined to the sky. There was a sense of independence in the sight that he admired, as well as a bit of pride. The dark blue sky was striated with silky cirrus clouds as far as the eye could see.

Spring had been dry to date, and would hurt the newly planted grain crops if it continued moistureless. People would flock to the railway towns to receive the Federation's relief supplies that were stored there regularly and replenished from the port city. Only the die hards would stay on their homesteads and use up their own stores. Again, many would stay in the towns; slowly the planet's culture would continue to change; the way of life for whose sake the planet was first settled would have to co-exist with newer ambitions.

He was more than four thousand kilometres from the port, on the single rail line that crossed the major continent. In addition to the two other continents, there was a group of large islands in the western ocean; most of these lay below the equator and were of volcanic origin. One day in the distant future, this large continent around him would break up and the pieces would drift away from each other. It was a young world, too young for native intelligent life. Much of the larger animal life had been killed off thousands of years ago, when the early colonists had arrived, during the first wave of interstellar expansion. The grass on the plain before him was originally from earth, as was much of the vegetation, though he had been told there were native forests still flourishing untouched on the islands.

Most of the human population lived on the coastal plains, east and west, joined by this rail line. The northland was too cold, the south too hot. The central plains supported a third of the planet's twenty million people on an area of one hundred million square kilometres; the costal settlements, with their fisheries and small farms supported the other two thirds. The seasonal contrasts were milder on the coast, more severe on the plains.

Whenever the train slowed, Kurbi had the urge to jump off and head for the nearest house; although he had met hundreds of people in family groups, he was still curious to see how the next group lived, how they would receive him. It meant that he would have to live with them until another train came through, to carry him further west or back to the port, but he did not mind; for a time his past life would again seem far away, almost as if it had never existed. The people here lived in a great religious dream of world and sky and growing things. He could enter into their lives, and leave at any time. A part of him knew that he was using New Mars to bury his past, but he did not care; that he felt better was enough. *All the past lives in the Federation corridor*, he thought, *worlds exist at every stage of development and its variation, each experiment and utopian scheme strives to continue, each failure struggles to survive.*

As the train slowed to a safe speed, Kurbi threw his

rucksack out ahead of him and jumped to the grass, rolling on the gentle slope. He got up, picked up his rucksack and crossed the east-bound tracks, walking back towards the house he had passed earlier.

The house was further away than he thought. After an hour of walking, it still seemed distant, as if defying him with its peaceful appearance. He stopped and sat down on the grass to rest. A cooling breeze passed across his back. He turned and saw the rain clouds sweeping towards him from the other side of the tracks like a curtain being drawn across the plain. Dark clouds were slipping over the horizon, bringing the much needed rain at last. When he saw lightning brighten the prairie with its pale flash, he got up and continued towards the house.

The rain caught him while he was still a quarter kilometre from the house. The sky flashed and the thunder rumbled, vibrating the ground. A bolt hit the grass a hundred metres to his right. He wiped the rainwater from his face as he ran, tasting its freshness on his lips; the smell of ozone was distinct as he drew a deep breath and quickened his pace.

The door of the house opened when he reached it, startling him. He stopped for a moment, then went inside.

Three women sat at a wooden table. A man closed the door and sat down at the head of the table.

'You are welcome,' the oldest looking woman said.

'Thank you – I'm dripping water all over your floor.'

'It will run through the boards,' the man said. Kurbi looked at him now. His hair was black and his eyes brown; he sat with his elbows on the table. All four people wore the same expression as the man, a look of tolerant interest. 'You are the offworlder,' the man added.

'How did you know?'

'From the rail town, from those who run the train. Are you the only one?'

'I think so,' Kurbi said. 'You've never met an off-worlder?'

'We have not,' the man said as if he were proud of the fact.

Kurbi took a step forward. 'My name is Rafael Kurbi.'

Thunder followed, lending an absurd portentiousness to his introduction.

'I am here with my wife and daughters. We do not exchange names with strangers . . . but since you have told me yours and do not know our ways, you may call me Fane Weblen.'

'I understand,' Kurbi said. The two younger women seemed to smile at him from behind their long, brown hair. The mother was without expression. Her chiselled, sun darkened features seemed bare with her hair put up in a bun on her head. Kurbi noticed the winding grey streaks.

'Please sit down,' she said in a decisive tone of voice, as if she resented his scrutiny.

Kurbi sat down in the one chair on the empty side of the table.

'Are you hungry?' she asked. 'We have eaten, but there is a little meat left.'

'No thank you, I ate on the train,' Kurbi said patting his rucksack which he held on his lap. 'When does the next train come by?'

'About a week,' Fane said, 'going east.'

'You don't like the train, do you?'

'No.'

'It takes from us our reliance on our bodies,' the older woman said.

'But isn't it useful?' Kurbi asked.

'When?' Fane said.

'Why – when someone is sick and needs a hospital . . .'

'We are never sick,' the woman said, 'unless it is time to die.'

'What about when the food is scarce?'

'To be useful is not always to be right,' Fane said. 'We know that is not the way on other worlds.'

The storm was dying outside. Kurbi turned and saw the light in the window brightening.

'The rain will help,' Kurbi said.

'It is welcome – but it is not enough,' Fane said.

'How old are your daughters?' Kurbi asked.

'They are spoken for,' Fane said.

'Do you have any sons?'

'They have gone.'

'Where?'

'To the port, the rail towns – we don't know,' Fane said.

Kurbi thought of his co-workers in the port, especially Den, who must have come from a family like this. A severe conflict would one day develop on New Mars, between those who would modernize according to Federation ways and those who would cling to the ideals of the original colonists. The conflict was even present in how Fane spoke to him. Quite clearly, he disapproved of offworlders and their influence, but his curiosity as well as good manners prevented him from showing his feelings overtly.

'How old are you?' the woman asked.

Her husband gave her a quick look of surprise and cut her off with another question. 'How long do people live where you come from?'

'I'm from earth,' Kurbi said, 'I'm forty two earth

years old. That's about thirty five of your years, which are longer. Federation citizens can live as long as they wish, depending on whether there is a rejuvenation facility nearby. Medical care is part of Federation Citizenship, a right. Technically, New Mars is part of the Federation, but it's up to you what you import.'

'Not every world has interstar transport facilities,' Fane said.

'That's true,' Kurbi said. He estimated that Fane was about fifty earth years old, but he looked older.

'But I have no wish to live beyond my time,' Fane added quickly, as if saying what was required of him to be rid of it. Then he looked directly at Kurbi and asked, 'Don't you wish to die?'

'Sometimes – many of my people take their own lives when it comes to that.'

'It was meant to be,' the woman said, 'the merciful God made the world to test us for another life, not for us to be happy in. If we are happy we will not learn what will be required of us later.'

'How long will you live?' Fane asked.

'I don't know – past a century, at least, I suppose. My . . . wife . . . died in a flying accident recently.'

'Flying?' Fane asked.

'Gliding – for sport.'

'I don't understand,' Fane said.

The woman shook her head but did not speak.

'That is why you are travelling?' Fane asked.

Kurbi nodded. 'May I stay here for a day or two? I've been doing chores for my food and a place to sleep. Can you use the help?'

'Yes, I can,' Fane said. Kurbi sensed that the mention of Grazia's death had affected Fane, perhaps reminding him of the certainty of his wife's death, as well as his own.

'You may stay until the next train, young man,' Fane's wife said. 'You may call me Slifa while you are with us.'

'And your daughter's names?'

Slifa looked to her husband. Fane shrugged.

'They are Azura and Apona,' she said.

'Twins?'

'Yes – they were made by God so that they might better see their own faults in each other.'

The two girls nodded solemnly at Kurbi, but he was still unable to see their full faces. He wondered if they were shy, or if they were supposed to wear their hair like a veil.

'I'm glad to know you, Azura and Apona.'

'You must not speak of knowing them,' Fane said.

'I see.'

'You must not look at them long,' Slifa added, 'they must not become accustomed to the gaze of any other except the ones who have spoken for them.'

'Very well.'

Fane got up and went to the fireplace, where he added two chunks of peat to the flames. 'You will sleep by the fire,' he said without turning around.

Silently, the women got up. Azura and Apona went to a door at the end of the room, opened it and disappeared into a dark room, closing the wooden door firmly behind them. Slifa went to the door at the opposite end of the room at Kurbi's right, opened it and went inside, leaving it slightly ajar.

Fane prodded the fire a few times with a stick, set it down finally and turned to take Slifa's chair across the table from Kurbi.

'Why are you really here, offworlder?'

'You're certainly curious about how people live elsewhere. I'm here for the same reason.'

Fane shrugged and his dark eyebrows went up. 'What is there to know – we know, and we know our way is right.' There seemed to be a suppressed anger in the man's manner, as if the existence of other worlds were an insult to him. 'I do not believe there are as many worlds as some say – certainly there are not as many as grains of sand.'

Kurbi did not answer, but searched for something else to say. 'I'd like to watch your sunset before I sleep,' he said finally.

Fane looked at him and smiled, relieved that Kurbi had not contradicted him about something he was unsure about. 'Yes – but the wind gets cold,' he said as he stood up. 'I will leave you now.'

'Sleep well,' Kurbi said as the man went into his bedroom and closed the door. Kurbi heard him putting something against the door inside.

There was a muffled giggle from the bedroom at his left as he stood up to go outside. When he opened the outside door he heard a faint squeak behind him, a door opening and closing suddenly.

Outside, the storm was completely gone. At his right the sky was clear and blue, darkening into jet black. The twin suns were balls of molten metal, joined with a white hot streamer of plasma. The wind from the east was cold, but there was less dust on its breath after the rain.

The suns touched the horizon and sank into the flat earth, until only an upward wash of red light was left. Abandoned, the planet seemed to shudder as the wind quickened and became colder. Kurbi turned and went back inside, closing the wooden door as quickly as possible behind him.

He unrolled his sleeping pack by the fire, put his package of provisions aside, and lay down by the warming flames. For a time he wandered in the suburbs of sleep, circling the centre of rest while images of his travels came to him like actors paying curtain calls.

'If you don't return in some months,' Nicolai had said, 'I'll take the flyer we have and come out along the rail line looking for you – so don't wander too far from the tracks.'

'I can take care of myself.'

'I will come anyway.'

'Suit yourself, Nico – you just want an excuse to travel, or is it because you'll miss our talks?'

'Both.'

'I'll get back, don't worry. If you feel so constricted, why don't you leave New Mars, start a new life elsewhere?'

'My family is here – I haven't faced the idea of leaving my parents permanently, not to go worlds away.'

'You don't have a wife or children.'

'No – there is a brother I haven't seen for years. It's not the same for me, Raf, as it is for you.'

'I think I understand. It would be as if the earth were not there anymore, as if something had destroyed it.' He had thought of the Herculean at that moment, of Julian and his offer, and it all seemed to mean more.

A bit of moist peat crackled in the fire, jarring him into wakefulness. He felt that eyes were watching him. The floorboards creaked under him as if someone were walking across the room towards him. The earth trembled under his back slightly and he sat up, wide awake.

The house shook a little, and the window facing east brightened. Kurbi stood up just as Fane came out of his bedroom. 'Do you have earthquakes?' Kurbi asked.

Fane shook his head and went out the door. Kurbi followed him outside. Together they watched the eastern sky glow brighter, burning with a blue-white light that rose higher and higher, as if the planet had disgorged a bolt of light to strike the sky. The horizon flashed once, twice; the ground shook again.

'What can it be?' Kurbi asked.

'I have never seen anything like this,' Fane said.

13. OCEAN STRIKE

'I balanced all, brought all to mind,
The years to come seemed waste of breath,
A waste of breath the years behind
In balance with this life, this death.'
– W. B. Yeats

The rock became a point and disappeared into the atmosphere of New Mars. A glow appeared against the blue ocean as the asteroid hurtled in at nearly one hundred kilometres per second, a forty billion ton missile that would strike the ocean just off New Marsport in less than a minute. The air glowed blue from the passage a few moments before impact.

Gorgias realized that he would not be able to see the full magnitude of the ocean strike from this distance.

'Describe what is happening,' he told the ship.

A violet flare appeared in the ocean below; it flashed once, twice.

SUB-NUCLEAR REACTION FROM HEAT OF IMPACT

The screen telescoped the distance until the area of ocean took up the whole screen.

OCEAN VAPOURIZED AT IMPACT POINT. CRUST PENETRATION THROUGH MANTLE. MAGMA EXPOSED.

Steam clouds covered the impact area, but the infrared glow of the wound in the ocean floor showed up clearly on the screen. The ocean was rushing in to cool that glow, creating the steam cloud that would soon veil the whole planet.

EFFECTS:
QUAKES,
OSCILLATION OF ALL PLANETARY WATER RESULTING
IN TIDAL WAVES.
HIGH WINDS,
RAINSTORMS.
DURATION INDEFINITE.

On the edge of the continent, the city of New Marsport glowed in the infrared sensors. Suddenly it was gone as the tidal wave covered it. The sensors continued to pick up the city's fading heat as the waves cooled it. And so it would be with every coastal settlement on the planet, as the angered ocean broke its gathered rage upon the shores, rolling in to reclaim its places until stopped by high ground and mountain ridges.

CLIMACTIC FORECAST:
INDEFINITE WINTER RESULTING
FROM CLOUD COVER.
RAIN AND WINDSTORMS INCREASING IN SEVERITY.
RECURRING TIDAL WAVES, TYPHOONS,
TORNADOES, WATERSPOUTS.
SUNLESS WORLD.

All this, he thought, from the energy released by the ocean's quenching of the strike heat. A ringed waterfall as high as a mountain range was rushing in to fill the hell hole of the impact, water and steam distributing the heat energy necessary to threaten the biosphere of a world. An economical weapon, he thought, wondering if he would use it again. If he announced his responsibility for the strike, it would be difficult to repeat this form of attack; yet he wanted them to know that he had done it, rather than some mindless natural process.

'Send a message,' he said to the ship, 'tell them we were here.'

In a few moments the communication would reach the exit beacon's warp transmitter-repeater; within minutes the Federation would know. He got up from his station and went aft to find his father.

All through the next day wind and rain swept across the plain. Kurbi and the Weblen family huddled in the small cellar of the house. The roof of the one storey house had been ripped off. Kurbi feared that the cellar would flood, forcing them out into the open, where survival in the wet cold would be impossible.

The twin girls and their mother huddled together in one corner of the wood-lined basement. Kurbi and Fane each sat in a different corner, facing the women.

'What is happening, offworlder?' Fane asked in the gloom, sounding as if he thought that Kurbi might be responsible for the disaster.

'I don't know – a volcanic eruption somewhere on the planet, maybe a large meteor strike. There's no way I can find out.' He wondered if Nicolai was safe.

'My spring crop is dying,' Fane said, 'nothing will grow. We are being judged.'

'Death is near,' Slifa said, 'we must compose ourselves.' Apona and Azura whimpered at her words.

'I – I can't accept this to be the will of God,' Fane said.

'Do not blaspheme,' Slifa said.

Thunder cracked as she spoke the words. She wailed and her daughters joined in.

'Be still,' Fane shouted over the wind and thunder, 'be still!'

'They can't help it,' Kurbi said, 'I'm fearful also.'

'You – afraid?'

'Yes.'

'Then we are lost.'

Suddenly more water began to flow into the cellar. In a minute they were in water up to their thighs.

'Up into the house,' Kurbi shouted over the rushing sound.

One by one they climbed the ladder into the roofless house. Here the fireplace was a mass of wet stones; chairs, pots and pans were scattered over the floor. Overhead, the sky drove with an unbroken obscurity of rain and dirt scooped up from the land.

'Over there,' Kurbi said, 'There's still some cover left in that corner. Help me with the overturned table – the women can get under it if we put it against the wall.'

They shoved the table into the corner and the three women crawled under it. Kurbi and Fane crouched on either side. 'If the walls blow away,' Fane shouted to him across the tabletop, 'we'll be done.'

'As long as there's a bit of wall,' Kurbi answered, 'there's hope.'

'What if the rain doesn't stop?'

'It will,' Kurbi said, 'it will.' *It must*, he said to himself, *or the plain will flood and sweep us away. The land can only absorb so much.*

'What time do you think it is?' Fane shouted.

There was no way to tell. The cloudcover had wiped out all distinction between day and night, morning and afternoon. Kurbi peered around the dark, debris strewn and water beaten floor, looking for his bedroll and rucksack.

Miraculously, the rucksack lay in the ruined fireplace, pinned down by a few stones that had fallen in from the chimney. Slowly he crawled over to the rucksack and dragged it backwards to the table.

Pulling out a few pieces of dried food, he handed them to the women under the table.

'Eat it – it's wet but we don't have much else.' The stores in the basement were under water now; this was all the food that was left. Hands reached out and took what he offered.

'Pass some to Fane,' he shouted.

He bit into the last piece himself, savouring the texture of synthetic protein and fruit flavour.

The light grew darker, until he could no longer see his own hands in front of his face.

I am a soldier, he thought, *my son is a terrorist.*

Everything was perfectly clear now. *If this is what it takes to survive and regain power, then I want no part of it.* A planet was dying nearby, and he had done nothing to prevent it. He would not be able to live with that knowledge.

He remembered Gorgias and Myraa playing as small children, with Oriona and himself looking on. The General would have been happy to know that his daughter, Myraa, had survived . . .

The old Herculean closed his eyes and lay still, overcome by the past. It was a sweet breeze of memory, enveloping him with longing and regret; he did not have the strength to struggle against it . . .

Gorgias, his brother Herkon and Myraa ran through the tall grass shouting and laughing. Oriona was smiling . . .

He should never have brought his son to the base, or

taken him on sorties; he should never have let him use the ship's library, or taught him the roll of destroyed worlds; he should never have believed the stories of a Herculean army still at large somewhere, regardless of the evidence that such an army had escaped through the ruined gate on Myraa's World. He had failed; his whole civilization had failed. If it were to grow back, it would have to do so slowly, peacefully, out of sight of its enemies, who now lived inside it in the form of hatred and the thirst for revenge. Perhaps there were irreversible things, and the Herculean Empire would never return, except maybe as something else . . .

Myraa, Gorgias and Herkon ran naked into his open arms, shapes out of time . . .

'Herkon is dead,' Oriona said one day, 'the others have taken him.'

'How?' he heard himself ask very long ago.

'Gorgias threw a rock against his head . . .'

His father was not in the aft cabin.

Gorgias turned and went forwards again to the control room.

'Am I alone?' he asked the ship.

YES.

'When was the lock opened?'

ONE HALF HOUR AGO.

'Scan nearby space.'

SCANNING. LIFEFORM AT SIX KILOMETRES.

'Overtake,' Gorgias said.

The disfigured face of New Mars disappeared, to be replaced by the sight of his father and scooter directly ahead. Gorgias went aft, put on his suit and stepped into the lock. It cycled and opened just as the ship came alongside the scooter.

Gorgias reached out and pulled the scooter inside.

As the lock closed and cycled, the figure toppled from the seat, pulled down by the ship's artificial gravity. The inner door opened and Gorgias pulled his father inside.

When he took off the helmet, he saw that the face was disfigured by lack of air pressure, eyes bulging wide open. Gorgias looked into the eyes as if he were looking across light years, hoping that far away, at a greater distance than he had ever known, something of his father might still be alive to be recalled by a sheer act of will.

Slowly, mechanically, he stood up and took off his own suit, then his father's, and hung them up in their places on the bulkhead.

Turning back to the body, he stared at it for a long time.

Finally he kicked it.

'You were waiting to do this,' he said, 'to take what remained of the past from me.' He knelt down and punched the discoloured face with his fist. 'Coward!' For a moment the mouth seemed to turn up into the semblance of a smile, but the flesh would not stay and it turned into a sneer. Gorgias raised his fist again and broke the nose with one stroke. 'You're nothing now – you've always been nothing. Why else would you have come to this, old man?'

A wild thought came into his mind. Myraa could drag his father back, make him face what he had done, if what she said was true. Would the broken nose make a difference, the frozen eyes an obstacle? He picked up the body and carried it into the aft cabin, and turned the temperature down to its lowest setting, insuring that the body would not begin to decompose for a while.

He rushed forward into the control cabin, sat down at the station and screamed an order.

'Switchover – evasive route to Myraa's World – we're being pursued by Federation cruisers.'

YOU ARE MISTAKEN,
NOTHING IS VISIBLE.

He would tell Myraa that the patrol ships had appeared just after he and his father had finished attaching the gravitic units to the rock. His father had been hit by laser fire, but he had managed to get him back into the ship before he died.

'Follow orders – Myraa's World,' he added.

When the ship was in jumpspace, Gorgias went aft and looked at his father's corpse floating in the zero-g field.

'I'll lose them,' he said, 'I'll get us home.'

Myraa will know what to do.

He went forward again and sat down at the screen station.

The grey continuum was clear; he was safe.

Closing his eyes, he tried to push away the nagging fear that came into him. His father was dead . . . honourably, he told himself, rehearsing the lie that would have to be told.

Myraa will know the truth, another part of him said.

Myraa will know what to do, his hopes whispered.

It was unthinkable for anything else except the lie to be true.

On the third day the rain slowed to a drizzle and some light came into the sky, a pitiably feeble glow that was put to shame by the more distant lightning flashes. Kurbi opened his eyes and found himself staring at the lighter sky for a long time.

'Slifa is dead,' Fane said, his voice seeming loud now

in contrast to the steady rush of the endless rain. 'The cold was too much for her.' Azura and Apona were crying softly.

As Kurbi watched the sky, he saw a black shape appear on the horizon. He stood up, pulling the wet blanket around him, and peered through the large hole in the east wall of the house.

'There,' he said pointing, but Fane and the twins paid him no attention.

The flyer came closer. *Nico*, Kurbi whispered and started towards the open doorway. He could not remember when the door had been blown away.

Kurbi leaned against the doorjamb and watched as the flyer came in low over the rails, casting a strong beam of light onto the rail bed below it. In a moment it veered from the railroad and approached the house, floating in to a gentle landing a hundred metres away on the windswept prairie.

A lone figure got out and walked towards him. Kurbi shivered as he recognized Nico's stocky frame. He stumbled a few steps forwards to meet him.

'Kurbi,' Nicolai Rensch said as he grasped Kurbi around the wet blanket, 'I knew you would be alive.'

Kurbi embraced him and the other steadied him on his feet with a strong grip.

'What has happened, Nico?' he managed to ask.

'Something hit the ocean off the coast. When the storm and tidal wave warnings came, I had only a few minutes to leave.' He shook his head and looked at the ground. 'I was not able to save anyone – if I had tried, they would have mobbed the flyer. I decided to look for you and help where I could do so safely and effectively. Is anyone else alive here?'

'A father and two daughters. The mother died of exposure last night . . .'

'The flyer has a good cabin, food and medical supplies – let's take them inside and warm up.'

Kurbi dropped the wet blanket from his shoulders and led the way back into the ruin of the house. There he pried the sobbing Fane away from the body of his wife and led him out towards the open lock of the flyer. Nico roused the twin girls out of their state of semi-shock and followed behind him.

Halfway to the black egg shape of the flyer, Fane stopped and stared at the light coming out from the lock. Turning, he grabbed Kurbi's arm and looked at him with hollow eyes. 'Where are we going – what is this fearful thing you have brought me to, offworlder?' Fane's face and body trembled.

'There's food and warmth inside,' Kurbi said, 'we'll be safe, don't worry. My friend Nicholai came from the port and found us.'

'Friend?' Fane's eyes were wide circles of darkness. 'What do you know of this devil? From the city? We should not accept help after God has punished us so much . . .'

Fane collapsed into his arms and Kurbi dragged him into the flyer.

'We can wander the planet,' Nicolai said, 'picking up survivors until the freighter from earth arrives.'

They sat in the control room of the flyer. On the screen the rain was coming down again and the landscape was almost completely dark. Fane and his daughters were in the mid-section cabin. All three had recovered somewhat after drying out and eating some food.

'There's no link with Federation on the planet?' Kurbi asked.

'There was in New Marsport – but that's . . . gone, under water.'

'Are the electrical storms affecting communications badly?'

'Pretty badly,' Nico said.

'Then we'll have to get the flyer up into orbit,' Kurbi said. 'From there we can talk to the subspace beacon station – it'll relay a message to the nearest Federation base.'

'Can you get us into orbit?' Nico asked.

'I think I can, if I study the flyer. It's the only way to get help here quickly. If we have to, we'll dock with the beacon station – there's a small installation inside, with provisions and first aid supplies, but I don't think we'll have to try that.'

'Let me show you something,' Nico said. He reached over and pressed a few control areas under the screen.

A picture appeared. 'I recorded this before heading west,' Nico said. A column of blue air stood in the ocean. At its base the ocean was turning into steam. 'It was huge,' Nico said, 'it went up through the whole atmosphere. Something came in from space and hit us hard, Raf.'

'How far away were you when you recorded this?'

'It sat on my horizon – I didn't want to get closer.'

14. SWIMMER IN SHADOWS

caught within ourselves
feeding inner hounds
in too tight a wood
we await the dawn

– Tymoteusz Karpowicz

In the polar mountains of Myraa's World, Gorgias waited on a glacier. Cold white light filled the cabin through the screen. There was no sign of pursuit vessels appearing near the planet. The ship was safe; he was safe.

As he waited, Gorgias made a vow of vengeance against the earthborn; he swore it to his father, to the twenty war stars of home and their dead worlds. The oldest Herculean had not died by his own hand; the Federation had killed him, as it had murdered his mother and brother, by exile.

He thought of his father lying cold in the aft quarters, waiting for his funeral . . .

'We're safe,' he said to the ship, 'take us to Myraa.' For a moment he felt brother to the ship, though it never spoke to him except through the screen readouts. He could order it to speak in a voice, now that he would be alone. *It will be strange to live now that my parents are dead, when all that was in them is in me, and nowhere else.* Whatever intelligence was buried in the vessel was also Herculean; it would die if he died; it would live as long as he lived.

The ship rose from the tilted icefield, revealing the sun suddenly at one end of the glacier, where it had been setting until the ship's lifting gave the illusion of sunrise.

Running east, the ship reached the glacier's edge and rushed out low over the ocean, whipping up whitecaps in its wake.

'He cannot be saved,' Myraa said.

As the sun set, the trees and grass in front of the house seemed to become drenched with blood; then slowly the darkness turned the red to black.

'Why not?' Gorgias asked as he turned from the windows to face Myraa.

'He cannot enter our circle because he has already become nothing. He died too far away, Gorgias, in distance as well as in belief. He got what he expected – eternal nothingness.' She paused. 'I have saved many of our dead, but I can do nothing for him.' She paused again. 'I warn you, Gorgias, die near me – it will be the only way I can save you.'

'My father was right, this is all nonsense – you can't frighten me.'

'I know how he died, Gorgias.'

'Stay out of my mind!'

He turned from her to the window, anxious not to let her see that he believed her in any way. Herculean women might have been telepathic, his father had once told him, or simply observant.

Outside, the dark countryside of hills and grass was blazing now with a million fireflies, as if . . . invisible mourners carrying laser candles had gathered for a funeral. The mass of lights was concentrated in the meadow below the house, but a snaking S shape ran up the nearby hill to his right and over the top.

Gorgias stepped closer to the window and looked out at the procession of lights. A sprinkling of stars had fallen on the darkening land, and he felt the edges of pity pushing in at him, threatening to break his self control; beyond pity stood sorrow and guilt, avengers of the dead.

'Gorgias!'

He whirled to face her again, ready now to answer her reproaches.

'Ships are coming,' she said. 'I warn you to show you that I am not your enemy, and that I can examine the content of minds, even at a distance.'

He had expected her to blame him further for his father's death, to question again the manner of his death. Something in him had hoped that she would; instead she spoke idle prophecies.

'You will die one day, Gorgias – but remember to die here, remember . . .'

Contempt surfaced in him, contempt for his own weakness, blotting out pity, sorrow and guilt. He stepped up to Myraa's naked form and hit her across the face. 'Get away from me!' he shouted, 'little animals, that's what you are here, animals, fools and cowards.'

She only looked at him and said, 'I did not have to tell you that ships are coming.'

'Why did you, then? You want me to die, you said so. How would you know anyway?'

But he almost knew her answer. 'I can feel them hating you as they come in their ships,' she said. 'How many did you kill for them to hate you that much? That many? It makes their hatred almost rational.'

'It's war,' he said.

'What war?'

'They killed my – our world, and my father.'

'Your father killed himself.'

'Stop!'

'It's true –'

'They drove him into cowardice, they took his great strength – they killed him!'

'Who's the liar, Gorgias?'

He lunged at her, grabbing her by the throat; it was soft and yielding as he squeezed. Her eyes held him as if in a vice. Suddenly he let her go.

'You're not worth killing,' he said, hating himself for his continued weakness. She was too close to him, too much a part of his past to let die.

'The ships are nearer,' she said, 'you'd better go.'

He went past her and out the back entrance. The grass was wet on the dark hillside. Fireflies exploded into brightness around him like miniature suns; he slipped a few times before he reached the bottom of the hill. He jumped into the open side lock and went directly forward as the inner door closed behind him.

'The base,' he said and sat down at the screen station.

HUNTERS APPEARING IN ORBIT

'Get us out of here,' he shouted.

The ship lifted straight up through the atmosphere. Patrol cruiser positions registered on the screen, coming fast from dayside.

The Whisper Ship slipped into otherspace, but in a moment Gorgias saw signs of pursuit: black dashes in the greyness behind him. This chase would be a long one, he knew, but he would lose them; he would lose them because he had to, because any other outcome would be unthinkable.

Ten days after Kurbi and Nicolai had made orbit in the flyer, Julian Poincaré arrived with a cruiser and a dozen freighters loaded with emergency supplies. Nicolai led the freighter's lifeboats down to the tortured planet, where storms, earthquakes and tidal waves continued to rage, and where the coming fimbul winter would soon make life all but impossible for the survivors. Nico was going to try to convince as many people as possible to leave New Mars and settle elsewhere.

'It was the Whisper Ship,' Julian told Kurbi in the cruiser's stateroom.

'How do you know?'

'He announced it himself – hundreds of worlds picked up the details on their relays. Most of the corridor knows by now. It was a large rock he threw at us, Raf.'

'I should have guessed – my luck.'

'Are you going to help me now?'

'I'd like to help Nicolai for a while – though I can see myself waking up one morning, picking up a weapon and going out to kill that monster, except –'

'What?'

'I want to see him alive – what kind of living being can destroy a planet and still live with itself?'

'He'd probably say you were taking it much too personally, since you lived through it. We did that to his world – once. Old injustices drive his life, or lives, whoever they are, and he dispenses new injustice. Who is to blame? Is there a good answer, or only answers that no one will like?'

'I would say there is no hope for them,' Kurbi said, '– too much past, as you say.'

Kurbi was silent for a moment. He looked around the stateroom, at the star maps covering the walls, at the green carpeting under his dirty feet, at Poincaré sitting behind the polished ebony desk. Kurbi sat down in one of the chairs in front of the desk and said, 'Julian, after what I saw down there, I think I will want to try and stop Gorgias.'

'Go home first, get some rest. We've got ships looking already – they may save you the trouble. You may not have the stomach to kill the Herculean, yet it may have to be done to stop him. For the terrorist, civilized behaviour is a screen. He counts on the enemy's inability to behave as he does.'

'You still think he's a good thing for us, Julian?'

'It wouldn't be the first time good came out of horror. Gorgias will keep us alert, interested; if we ignore him, he or his descendants will topple us one day.'

Suddenly Kurbi felt very tired. *Home*, he thought, but all he could visualize was his small room in New Marsport, and the various houses he had slept in during his travels.

'Where do you think the Whisper Ship has gone?' he asked, trying to concentrate.

'I think he's at Myraa's World – much of his audience for his deeds is there, a harmless bunch, really. But we won't find him there. He has a base somewhere, remember? He'll be there by then.'

Gorgias fled into the southern regions of the galaxy, reentering normal space and slipping back into bridgespace dozens of times; but still the hunters followed, making every turn, imitating every changeover.

After a week of travel there was no sign of the cruisers on the grey screen, but that was only because the Whisper Ship's slightly superior speed was finally giving him a lead. At any moment the black dashes would appear on the screen, marking the pursuit positions.

Gorgias waited. The ship was on its own – following any evasive manoeuvre that became practical. He closed his eyes and tried to get some rest.

The ship switched to normal space. There was still no

sign of the hunters, but directly ahead a white hot star was streaming a tail of material into space.

BLACK HOLE BINARY.
MATERIAL DISAPPEARING FROM NORMAL SPACE-TIME

The ship rushed towards the empty point in space where the whirlpool streamer of stolen star material ended. Gorgias noted the halo of debris circling the dead spot in space.

In a few minutes the ship passed the ring of captured matter and seemed to be heading directly towards the black hole.

'Explain,' Gorgias shouted, wondering if something had finally gone wrong with the ship.

EVASIVE MANOEUVRE:
PASSAGE THROUGH BLACK HOLE ERGOSPHERE
WILL SIMULATE DISAPPEARANCE.

ONE HOUR IN ERGOSPHERE, SHIP TIME, EQUALS ONE STANDARD GALACTIC MONTH.

HUNTER SHIPS LACK POWER FOR SKIRTING
BLACK HOLE EVENT HORIZON.

The ship dived, circled the dead spot in space for one hour while Gorgias waited. Half the sky was a black lake trying to pull him in, while in the bright universe of stars time was rushing past him at a furious pace. If the ship stayed here too long, all the history of the universe would pass by him; stars would grow old and die, all nature would become a ruin rushing together . . .

He got up and went to the aft cabin. His father's body hung motionless in the chilled air. He imagined a conversation between himself and the old Herculean:

'Get them for me son, never rest – promise!'

I will.

'You must hate them as much as I do.'

I do.

'If you are caught you must die.'

I will.

He knelt before the floating, laser burned body, and shivered in the cabin's cold air. A new peace came over him; he had made his vow; his father had asked him at last, and the vow was real.

In jumpspace view, the Hercules Cluster was a mass of black stars exploding outwards from a black centre.

Gorgias turned off the screen and dozed as the ship came home. There had been no sign of hunters after the black hole manoeuvre, and it was now too late for the pursuers to discover the direction he had taken; they might guess that his base was in the cluster, but it would take centuries to check each star.

When he woke up, he sensed that the ship was sitting in its berth. He got up, went to the aft quarters and carried his father's body out to the scooter. Securing the corpse in the back seat with a strap, he took the forward position and floated out through the open lock.

The base lights were steady as he whisked down the passageway towards the stasis chambers. His father leaned forward against him, cold and stiff, as the tunnel dipped into the deepest parts of the base. Gaining speed, Gorgias rushed into the underworld, emerging at last into a large circular chamber lit by one large globe of orange light.

Here the empty stasis shells stood in a circle around the room.

Gorgias stopped the scooter in front of one, took his father off the rear seat and pushed him into the shell. The field flickered as it received the body, surrounding it with a deep gloom. The shell would do as well as a tomb, he thought. He could barely make out his father's face as the darkness took him, hollowing his eyes into caves that stared out into the room. The old Herculean would remain as he was for as long as the base renewed itself, for as long as power fed the accumulators, for as long as his son's hatred lived; from here the old Herculean would command all that was to come.

When he stepped into the shell at his father's right hand, Gorgias knew that two decades would pass; he could set the return for much later, if he wished, but two decades would be enough to confuse the hunters further; he would disappear from their experience for a while, enough time for them to lose interest or let down their guard. In any case, when he emerged the search would be going slower and he would have the element of surprise.

To step into the stasis field and step out at any time in the future would always be a matter of a moment. He hesitated, thinking, *I never had a chance to grow up in my world, with millions like myself around me. I never had a chance to take what was mine . . .*

He stepped into a profound darkness, which became bright red.

Yellow leaves grew on trees nourished not by water but by blood; the soaked roots drank greedily, until the leaves curled scarlet and dropped to earth, each veined structure a world dying on the parched ground.

A bright sun turned the landscape white hot, until his eyes stared into white space. A raging wind whipped him, enveloped his body with icy fingers and hurled him against invisible obstacles. Hatred froze inside him, petrifying his bones and organs; a hot wind came and coursed fire through his heart and stomach.

He opened his mouth to protest but only curses emerged – words like wars hurled through the doors of speech . . .

He swam in the shadows, waiting for the iron game to resume.